Game Time

Married to the Game

Sherron Elise

Published by Sherron Elise, 2022.

Also by Sherron Elise

Married to the Game
Interference
Game Time

The Slumber Sisters
Think Fast
So Many Secrets
My Sisters' Keeper
The Christmas Wish
Differences
Crush
Copycat

Standalone
A Kiss From An Angel
All That Glitters
Rumorz
The Baby on the Doorstep
The Desire of Her Heart
The College Christian Chat 21 Day Devotional
Excess Baggage

Chapter One

Tatum Addison executed a perfect herkie into the air just as the buzzer sounded, signaling the end of the game and sealing the UCLA Bruins' fate as the new NCAA champions. The roar from the sold-out crowd inside the Alamodome was thunderous. Tatum was radiant with pride for her school as well as for her man, the Bruins' star player, Kingsley Watts. She couldn't help but laugh as King and his teammates hugged and roughhoused in celebration of their victory against the Duke Blue Devils until a *SportsCenter* reporter managed to garner King's attention and pull him away for an impromptu post-game interview.

As blue and gold confetti rained down upon them, Tatum left her fellow cheerleaders behind and bumped her way through the throngs of people to stand near King and his family as he was interviewed. His handsome features were a mask of concentration as he struggled to hear the reporter's questions amid the frenzy on the court. His mother, Michelle, gave Tatum a huge smile and a hug as Tatum joined them while his father, Jacoby, was focused intently on his son's interview. Before she could give King a congratulatory kiss, he was whisked away to the stage that was erected mid-court for the trophy presentation. Tatum thought she would go blind as more confetti rained down upon them from the blasters positioned on both sides of the stage. The arena looked like a snowstorm of blue and gold.

Once the crowd settled, King took the mic, and the presenter asked him about a repeat performance for his upcoming senior year.

"Unfortunately, this will mark my last year as a Bruin. I have decided to forego my senior year and enter the upcoming NBA draft."

The arena erupted into loud rumbles of applause and excitement at King's announcement, but Tatum went numb from shock. King was leaving college early to go pro? Why hadn't he shared this news with her before sharing it with the world? She zoned out and watched the remainder of the presentation on autopilot. Once the team began exiting the podium, heading toward the locker rooms, Tatum finally willed her feet to move forward and went to approach King, but she lost him within the hysteria of reporters shouting more questions at him as they trailed him into the locker room.

Tatum was surprised that her cousin, Gya Lawson, managed to find her within the midst of the celebratory mayhem. Gya had driven in from Texas A&M, booking a room within the same hotel where the cheerleaders were housed. She didn't want to miss out on supporting her favorite cousin and her man in their championship run.

Gya pulled her in for a hug. "Girl, King was a beast out there tonight."

"I'm gonna kill him," Tatum said through gritted teeth. "Can you believe he announced he's going pro without telling me a single word?"

Gya's soft brown eyes widened. "Are you serious? Well, maybe he wanted it to be a surprise."

"You surprise the *world* with this type of life-changing news, not your girlfriend of three years."

"Look, just try to calm down. Don't ruin this celebration," Gya tried to soothe.

"The team discussed heading over to The Rooftop if we won the championship, and a few of us cheerleaders planned on joining them," Tatum said. "It's gonna be hard for me to keep a smile plastered on my face all night. King has some explaining to do."

"That can wait, Tatum. Just try to put it in the back of your mind for right now."

"Why don't you come and hang out with us? I'm sure King will be happy to see you."

Gya looked hesitant. "Tay, you know I don't do nightclubs."

"The Rooftop is an upscale sports lounge, and you don't even have to stay long. C'mon, Gya. I could really use a buffer between me and King tonight."

Gya agreed, and they headed to her vehicle to drive back to the hotel so Tatum could shower and change. Due to the massive amount of traffic outside of the arena, it took them nearly thirty minutes to finally arrive. Gya followed Tatum to the room she shared with a fellow cheer mate, Julie, who wasn't inside, so Tatum figured she'd headed straight to the lounge. Tatum showered while Gya flipped through channels on the television, and soon thereafter, they were heading back to the car and driving to The Rooftop.

Blaring music and dim purple, yellow, and green lighting from a strobe greeted them when they entered. Several flat-screen televisions aligned the bar area where Tatum could see King featured on *SportsCenter*, speaking into a mic at the post-game press conference.

Tatum groaned. "Oh great. If the press conference is still going on, that means King hasn't even showered yet. It could be forever before he arrives."

"I'm only staying an hour, Tatum," Gya reiterated.

"Fine, fine," Tatum said, flagging down a passing waitress.

She ordered a frozen margarita while Gya requested a bottle of Perrier water. They found available seats on a sofa, and after a few sips of her drink, Tatum felt herself start to relax. She and Gya chatted, looking on at the other patrons who had made their own dance floor in the center of the lounge. Tatum joined in as they began to do The Wobble. After about an hour, Tatum was still grooving on the makeshift dance floor but became distracted by a commotion. She watched as a group of women made their way toward the entrance. Straining her neck to see what was going on, she realized The Bruins had finally arrived. King was standing front and center.

The DJ cued up Run-D.M.C.'s "Down with the King." Tatum watched, appalled as two women brought a chair to the center of the lounge and had King sit, then they proceeded to gyrate their bodies in front of him. King took it all in, grinning like a Cheshire cat. When one of the women straddled King to give him a lap dance, Tatum had seen enough.

"Oh, hell no." Tatum made her way over to her man, and Gya was on her heels to keep her cousin from doing something crazy.

King glanced up, smiling at Tatum. "Hey, baby. Join in and show 'em how it's done," he encouraged.

"Boy, you done lost your mind." Tatum grabbed an empty beer bottle from a nearby table and smashed it against the table's edge. She held the sharp edge of the broken bottle to King's throat.

Gya intervened, grabbing her arm. "Tay, stop. Calm down."

"Yeah, bae. What's your problem?" King said, glaring at Tatum as he inched away from the imposing sharp object.

A crowd had formed around them, and several people were recording on their cellphones.

"She's seriously trying to kill him." One of the girls who'd gyrated against King exclaimed.

Tatum threw what was left of the bottle in her direction, its remnants crashing to the floor and shattering just like her heart, as she made her way out of the sports lounge in a blind rage. Angry, hot tears streamed down her cheeks.

"Tatum, c'mon now. It's gonna be okay," Gya said, catching up with her. She opened her purse and removed a bottle of hand sanitizer. "Here. Take some of this. No telling who had their mouth on that beer bottle you picked up. Did you cut your hands? Tay, what were you thinking?"

"You see how he played me just now? Like a straight fool. Winning the championship and now this whole NBA business has already gone to his head. He made me look like a joke in there. That's not how you treat somebody you supposedly love, Gya." Tatum proclaimed, as tears of hurt and humiliation continued to flow.

Gya hugged her cousin as Tatum sobbed in her arms. Gya helped usher her back to the car.

"King's behavior tonight, coupled with the fact that he withheld his NBA draft news from me, makes me question where I fit into his future," Tatum said as they rode back to the hotel. "Besides, I want to complete my senior year and receive my degree, which means King and I will have a long-distance relationship."

"You need to finish college. I'm behind you one hundred percent on that," Gya said. "King is chasing his dreams, and you shouldn't have to give up on your own."

"Maybe I can relocate with him. Despite his antics tonight, I still love him, and I'm not staying in California and giving thirsty women free access to my man. You saw firsthand what I have to deal with. I've had to shoo away the thirsties since we first began dating. They're always bold enough to flirt with him right in my face, so there's no way I'm leaving him in a new city alone."

"I can honestly say I don't know what that's like. Bryant is always setting females straight and letting them know he's devoted to me."

Tatum felt a tinge of envy at the mention of Gya's fiancé, Bryant Green, Texas A&M's star running back, and it wasn't because she wanted Bryant for herself. It was because Gya was right. Bryant was truly devoted to her, and they were set to wed in less than two months. Tatum envied the commitment Gya sealed from Bryant. The four-carat princess-cut diamond ring adorning her finger seemed to shimmer and wink in the light of the moon that shined through the windshield of the car, as if taunting Tatum.

Tatum did admire the fact that Gya and Bryant were waiting to consummate their marriage on their wedding night, but she didn't share her cousin's willpower. She'd lost her virginity to King during their freshman year at UCLA, shortly after they first started dating. King even once stated that he found Bryant's stance on holiness rather corny.

"Yes. Why don't we change the subject and talk about your big day? Discussing King is not helping me keep my temper in check one bit. I bet you're real excited about walking down that aisle in a couple of months, huh?"

Gya's vanilla-toned features brightened. "Girl, yes. I'm so happy to be marrying my soulmate."

"Are you nervous about your wedding night?"

"Not at all. I'm looking forward to it."

"Gya, I hope I'm not out of line with this, but...how do you know if you and Bryant are...sexually compatible? What if he doesn't satisfy you in bed?"

"Tay, I'm not worried about that at all. I remember this women's Bible study I attended about a year ago, and it was discussed that when you meet your God-ordained husband, his male organ will be a perfect fit to your...womanly parts, I'll say."

Tatum frowned. "What? Girl, who said that nonsense?"

"I believe it. God knows exactly what I need to be satisfied by my husband physically and emotionally. Now I'm gonna need for you to raise up outta my bedroom," Gya said with a laugh.

Tatum shrugged and raised her hands in surrender. "Hey, I was just asking."

"Do you regret losing your virginity to King—I mean, not waiting until marriage at least?" Gya asked.

Tatum shook her head. "What I won't do, some other girl will. There's no way I could've kept going out with King without us making love."

"See, that's what I mean. Tatum...Don't take this the wrong way, but what if King is not the guy God has for you? Maybe him going to the NBA is a blessing in disguise."

Tatum's eyes widened. "What?"

"I mean, you just said it yourself: You don't trust him to be alone in a new city, and you felt you'd lose him if you didn't sleep with him. That's not the type of relationship I'd want to be in. It honestly sounds like you don't trust him."

Tatum rolled her eyes. "There you go. I knew it wouldn't be long before you got on your holy soap box. I'm sorry my relationship is not as pure as yours, oh-so-godly Gya."

"Don't even go there. And why are you getting so defensive? Look, I know you're still upset about King's announcement and what happened at the lounge, so I'm gonna let your little attitude slide."

Tatum rolled her eyes and decided to just spend the remainder of the drive in silence, reflecting over the dynamics of their family. Gya's mother and Tatum's father, Charles, were siblings, but since Charles and Tatum's mother, Vanessa, had never wed, Tatum always felt like an unwanted black sheep. Another thing she envied about Gya was the fact that Gya was the product of a loving two-parent household. Charles had not been happy about Vanessa's pregnancy and agreed to support Tatum financially, but he'd never sought to establish a true father-daughter relationship.

"Hey, was King's brother at the game tonight?" Gya asked, finally breaking the silence as they pulled into the parking lot of the hotel.

Tatum shook her head. "You remember I told you that Korey finally came out of the closet? King is embarrassed about having a gay brother, and their father is just as ashamed. I remember Mr. Jacoby jokingly telling King that Korey would probably get turned on by all the testosterone on the court, so it's probably best if he just stayed in Memphis."

"While I don't agree with them shunning and taunting him, you and I both know what the Bible says concerning homosexuality." Gya stated.

Tatum rolled her eyes and quickly gathered her purse before Gya went into another holy spiel. They entered the hotel and bid each other goodnight, heading to their separate rooms. Tatum realized she hadn't eaten anything since before the start of the game, but her stomach was twisted in knots from her anger at King showing his whole behind tonight. As Tatum walked inside of the empty hotel room, her thoughts were still on her beautiful but nerve-wracking cousin whom she'd looked up to since they were children. The two were only a year apart in age, and Tatum remembered being so impressed when Gya told her about meeting Bryant during cheerleader camp at Texas

A&M. Gya and Bryant crossed paths while he was in summer football training camp, and they'd been inseparable ever since.

Tatum also became a cheerleader a year later at UCLA, but she hadn't set her sights on any athletes. She'd become acquainted with King after signing up to be an athletic tutor for extra college credits. She initially begged off from King's advances. He was a very popular athlete, and she didn't need the headache that came along with dating someone of his caliber, but his charm eventually wore her down, and they'd fallen deeply in love. Tonight was the first time she'd questioned the strength of their relationship.

Tatum started to tear up again as she glanced over at the other empty double bed. Julie was still at the lounge and probably having a blast with King and the rest of the team. The show went on without her. Sighing, Tatum donned her PJs and drifted off into a restless sleep.

Chapter Two

Tatum was awakened by the ringing of her cell phone. She shot up and grabbed it, anticipating seeing King's photo flashing on the screen, but it was her mother, Vanessa's photo she saw instead. Tatum glanced over toward the other bed where Julie was slumbering. Tatum hadn't even heard her return to the room. Tatum took her phone and padded into the restroom so as not to awaken her.

"Baby, why didn't you tell me King was going pro?" Tatum could hear the excitement bubbling from her mom's voice. "I can't believe my daughter is about to be an NBA wife."

"Not so fast, Mom. I didn't tell you because he didn't even tell *me*."

"Well, I can't really blame him. You should keep big decisions like that under wraps. I guess he didn't want any leaks to the media," Vanessa reasoned.

"I would've never told anyone, Mom. King should know that."

"Tay, don't sweat the small stuff," Vanessa advised. "Just be happy that your man is about to be a million-dollar baller. I couldn't be prouder of my future son-in-law. Tell him I said congratulations when you catch up with him. I'm headed into work, so I'll talk to you later, Mrs. NBA."

After hanging up with her mother, Tatum slid back into bed and checked her phone for any missed calls from King. Finding none, her heart sank again. Tatum sent Gya a text asking if she was awake, knowing that Gya planned to be up early to drive back to College Station. Gya responded within minutes, and Tatum asked if she could drive her over to King's hotel. The Bruins players were housed in a much fancier hotel than the cheerleaders, but it wasn't located far. Gya agreed, and soon, they were headed to the Marriott Hotel.

Gya decided to stay in the lobby to give Tatum privacy to talk with King, but she cautioned Tatum to remain calm and not cause another scene. Tatum rode the elevator to the third floor and took a deep breath when she stood in front of Room 304. She and King had texted their hotel room numbers to one another when they arrived in San Antonio but due to game related obligations, they'd been unable to spend any quality time together. She knocked softly, and the door was opened by a sleepy-eyed Seth Walters, a power forward for the Bruins who was sharing a room with King.

"King's still sleep, Tatum," Seth said, rubbing at his eyes.

"I'm so sorry to have awakened you, Seth, but I really need to talk to him."

Seth sighed. "I'll see if I can rouse him."

Tatum paced outside the room for over five minutes. Soon, King emerged, his handsome features a mask of annoyance as he glared at her.

"What do you want, Tatum? You almost ruined one of the best nights of my life with your little beer bottle stunt, and now you're waking me up early in the morning knowing I have a flight to catch later."

"K–King, I came to apologize, and I hope we can talk things over."

"You know what really pisses me off?" King talked right over her as if Tatum hadn't even said anything. "I'm a national champion, and not once have you congratulated me. You know how selfish that is? And you better be glad the manager of the lounge didn't press charges against you for causing a disturbance."

Tatum's eyes welled with tears. King had never talked to her so harshly before, not even during their more heated arguments. She could tell he was very disappointed in her, and it hurt.

"Look, King, I'm sorry," Tatum said again and then felt embarrassed about groveling. She could only imagine how pathetic she sounded. "I'll admit it was selfish of me not to congratulate you on the championship, but my feelings were hurt when you made the NBA announcement, not even bothering to fill me in first. Can't you understand that?"

King's look of consternation deepened. "So that's what your funky attitude is about? Honestly, your behavior has me wondering if you're even ready to be an NBA girlfriend, much less a wife. Look, I need some space."

Tatum swallowed, feeling as if a golf ball was lodged in her throat. "King, what does that mean?"

"Exactly what I said. Give me some space."

"So, you're breaking up with me?"

"I don't know all that yet. I just need time to think. My life is changing rather fast, and I need to re-evaluate some things."

Tatum was done degrading herself. Mustering the last bit of dignity she had remaining, Tatum simply nodded and turned to leave, flinching as she heard King's door slam behind him.

Tears were streaming down her cheeks as she boarded the elevator again and met Gya in the lobby.

"I guess the conversation didn't go well?" Gya said. Tatum just laid her head upon her shoulder and Gya hugged her cousin long and hard. They then silently walked back to the car.

Gya drove Tatum back to her hotel, and Tatum told her to be careful during her drive back to College Station and to text her when she arrived safely. When Tatum returned to the room, she saw Julie awake and packing for their return flight to LA.

"Hey, Tatum. Last night was crazy, huh?" Julie said.

"Yeah, tell me about it," Tatum agreed absently as she started to gather her own things.

Julie started to say something else but then stopped, averting her sea blue eyes, and continuing to stuff her duffel bag.

Her hesitation didn't go unnoticed by Tatum. "Jules, what is it?"

"Your nasty confrontation with King is circulating on Twitter. I just want you to be forewarned that a few trashy gossip sites will pick up the story, if they haven't already."

Tatum groaned then sighed deeply. "I'm not surprised, and honestly, I should've known better."

"You know, I can't see how you deal with dating a star player like King. While I enjoy cheerleading, I know I'm too jealous to date a Bruins player. That's why I choose to stick with the nerdy bookworm types that worship the ground I walk on." Julie laughed.

Tatum managed a forced laugh along with her, but inside she quaked with anxiety. A lot of those gossip blogs such as The Daily Dish could be vicious, not to mention the nasty comments left by its readers. Tatum was probably being eaten alive for her behavior, and she had no one to blame but herself. She arrived in San Antonio full of hope and expectation for a championship win and was returning to LA with a smeared reputation and possibly a single woman.

***

Arriving back to campus after her three-hour drive from San Antonio, Gya napped and then had an evening dinner with Bryant. She checked on Tatum to make sure she made it safely back to LA. Tatum was still despondent, and King had not reached out since their morning confrontation. Gya resolved to keep her cousin in her prayers. Up bright and early the next morning with her Kierra Sheard playlist on full blast, Gya did a twirl in front of her full-length mirror, admiring her svelte figure in the white bodycon dress she'd chosen for the scheduled photo shoot and interview with *I Said Yes*. She and Bryant were being featured within the Christian online magazine that highlighted engaged and married couples living for Christ.

A knock at the front door interrupted her once-over. She walked out of her bedroom to open it and found her man standing on the other side, his six-one frame filling the doorway. Bryant looked so handsome in jeans, a white polo shirt, and a dark blue blazer. He flashed his trademark delectable grin. It always made her want to devour his lips whole, but she chastised herself for such ungodly thoughts. Man, she couldn't wait until their wedding night. It seemed like the temptation to be intimate with Bryant grew stronger with each passing day, but Gya knew that was nothing but a trick of the enemy. She wouldn't dare compromise when they were so close to sealing their union.

Gya fanned herself while flashing her fiancé a coy grin. Bryant pulled her into his arms for a soft and gentle kiss.

"All ready to go? The writer from the magazine said she would meet us outside of the Memorial Student Center."

Gya ran back into her bedroom to grab her clutch purse. She locked up the apartment and followed Bryant to his charcoal F-150 Ram truck. He'd been attached to this truck handed down to him by his father since his freshman year.

"Bae, as soon as you're drafted and sign the ink to your contract, we're upgrading to a Range Rover." Gya laughed as she buckled in for the short ride to the student center.

"No way you're getting rid of ole blacky here. This truck has character, baby," Bryant said with a wink.

Gya and Bryant soon met up with the magazine writer, Toshina, along with the photographer and videographer assigned to the feature. The group then made their way to the meditation room of the All Faiths Chapel where the interview would take place. Bryant's clout on campus enabled him to reserve the chapel for the duration of the in-depth conversation with the magazine.

"This interview will also be posted on our YouTube channel. After our talk, I'd like to head over to the Forster Courtyard and Garden to shoot some pics. I must say you two make a striking couple. I know we'll get some lovely shots to share with the world."

Both Gya and Bryant smiled, thanking her.

"Now, Gya, I've studied your social media pages, and you make it no secret that you are a virgin. Has it been difficult to refrain from sex?" Toshina dove right in and pulled no punches.

"Yes. I'm not going to lie and say it has been easy, especially considering the other females who try to throw themselves at Bryant, but our faith in God has sustained us."

"Bryant, how do you manage not to yield to temptation? You're one of the top-ranking running backs in the country and a Heisman trophy winner, not to mention you're one of the highest anticipated NFL draft picks."

"Like Gya said, it's God who keeps me humbled. I realize all the accolades you mentioned can disappear in a flash. Even though I lost my virginity in high school, Gya has really kept me in check during my years of celibacy. Not only that, but my mother has also taught me how to respect women. I have my parents' marriage as a glowing example." Bryant clasped Gya's hand and brought it to his lips.

"I know it may sound corny and cliché, but I feel like I'm the luckiest girl in the world to get married straight out of college to the love of my life. I'm living every woman's dream," Gya gushed.

"I understand that you facilitate a women's Bible study here on campus," Toshina probed.

"Yes," Gya said, beaming proudly. "It's called Well Worth the Wait, and I encourage other young females to abstain from sex and treat our bodies like the precious and pure pearl that they are. It's so refreshing to see how many of my peers want to be pure on their wedding night. I believe my stance is why God saw fit to present me to Bryant so soon. I've heard horror stories about women who are single well into their fifties. I believe God is rewarding my dedication and commitment to honoring Him and His Word."

Toshina raised an eyebrow. "So, you're saying the reason that so many women are still single is because they choose not to abstain?"

"Yes. I feel that has a lot to do with it. My mom and grandmother often quote an old saying: 'Why buy the cow when you can get the milk for free?' It saddens me to see so many women take a casual stance on sex. They leave these guys with nothing to look forward to. Having sex prematurely clouds your judgment, and your emotions become ruled by the lust of your flesh. Besides, I don't feel you're ever too young to be marriage minded. That's the purpose of my Bible study group."

"Besides your decision to abstain, what else sets your relationship apart from others?" Toshina asked.

Gya, now on a roll, spoke up before Bryant could part his lips to provide an answer. "Bryant and I *court* as opposed to dating. I believe dating is a worldly standard when it comes to relationships. Courting, on the other hand, is more serious and exclusive. You can date numerous people at one time, but courting holds more significance and meaning. Best of all, it's *God's* way."

"From the very beginning of our relationship Gya set boundaries," Bryant interjected. "This was something new to me because I was used to girls falling at my feet. For example, we've never stayed overnight with each other, always parting ways before nine p.m."

"So, no late-night study sessions?" Toshina asked with a grin.

Both Gya and Bryant laughed.

"Nope. I leave him with a goodnight kiss and return to the campus apartment to study my Bible," Gya stated.

After a few more questions, they went out to the courtyard and garden. It was a beautiful and sunny spring day that provided excellent lighting for the photo shoot.

"Okay, that will about do it. I have everything I'll need for this feature. The interview will be posted to our website and YouTube page in about a day or two. I enjoyed meeting and chatting with you and wish both of you the best," Toshina said.

Bryant and Gya thanked her for her professionalism. Wrapping his arm around Gya, he asked her about her plans for the rest of the day.

"I'm going to head back to the apartment for a quick afternoon nap. How about doing dinner later this evening?" Gya suggested.

"It's a date," Bryant agreed. He drove her back to her apartment, and they parted with a kiss.

Gya's roommate, Jocelyn, was in the kitchen enjoying an afternoon lunch from Subway when Gya entered.

"Hey, roomie. How did the interview go?"

"It was great," Gya responded, kicking off her heels. "I really enjoyed it."

Jocelyn nodded and gathered up her trash. "I'm about to head over to the registrar's office to make sure all of my paperwork is clear for graduation."

Gya snapped her fingers. "You just reminded me I need to make an appointment with the career center to spruce up my résumé. I also need to talk to a few of my professors about reference letters."

Jocelyn laughed. "Gya, are you serious right now?"

Gya frowned. "What do you mean?"

"Why are you worried about résumé and reference letters as if you really need to enter the workforce after graduation? Bryant will sign a contract next month that we all know will be worth millions. It's a blessing that you don't have to worry about a career after graduation. You know how many people that graduated last year are still living at home and looking for jobs?" Jocelyn pointed out.

"I've never planned on living off Bryant. I want us to both have successful careers. I plan to take Well Worth the Wait global."

"Yes, and I'm sure Bryant will invest in your entrepreneurial endeavor with no problems. See, that's what I mean. You can start your own business without even having to worry about startup costs and funding. You can work on your dreams daily without a second thought about how bills will be paid. *Humph,* must be nice," Jocelyn said, grabbing her purse and making her way toward the front door. "I'll catch up with you later."

Gya stood looking at the door, Jocelyn's words echoing within her head. When Gya thought about it, she realized she *was* very blessed, but she never wanted to come off like some gold digger. She truly loved Bryant and would still be just as happy to marry him if he worked a regular nine-to-five job after graduation.

She reflected on the day when Bryant had knocked her off her feet—literally—during cheerleader camp. He was warming up for practice with a jog when they collided with each other. Bryant had been so gentle and apologetic, helping her to her feet and walking her to the student health center, staying as her scraped knee was cleansed and bandaged. Later that evening, he'd sought her out in the Commons dining hall, sitting to eat with her. Before leaving, he'd gotten her cell phone number, and that was the start of their relationship. Her parents were smitten from the moment she first brought Bryant home, and the Greens adored Gya just as much.

Yes, the love she shared with Bryant was not something she ever took for granted, and she planned to use their marriage as a platform to further glorify Christ. The interview with *I Said Yes* was a great start.

Chapter Three

"Miss Addison, considering the recent video of you...in a not-so-flattering light, we are asking for you to step down from the cheerleading team, and I regret to inform you that due to you violating UCLA's code of conduct, you are ineligible to try out again for your senior year," UCLA's athletic director, Timothy Keller said, his face stern.

Bruins head cheer coach Karen Mulgrew sat looking somber as Tatum was delivered the heartbreaking news. She'd become filled with dread since receiving the text from Coach Mulgrew informing her Mr. Keller was requesting to see her in his office.

Tatum figured she'd be reprimanded for her actions at the lounge, but she had no idea she'd be banned from cheering again. At the very least, she'd expected a suspension. Too tired to argue, Tatum simply nodded and apologized to Mr. Keller for embarrassing the university. Tatum thanked Coach Mulgrew for everything and silently exited the office, but she paused when she heard the coach call her name, turning to see the petite woman hurrying to catch stride with her.

"Tatum, I'm so disappointed with the university's decision. Believe me, I fought hard for you. You're a great student and one of my brightest cheerleaders. I was really pushing for a suspension, but Mr. Keller had concerns that the incident placed the school in a bad light and diminished the accomplishment of our victory win."

"Coach Mulgrew, I understand," Tatum said, swallowing past the lump in her throat.

Coach Mulgrew hugged her. "Will you still attend the victory parade downtown tomorrow?"

Tatum shook her head. "No. I think I just need to be by myself for a while and regroup."

"Well, I'm here if you need to talk, sweetheart," Coach Mulgrew assured.

Tatum numbly made her way back to her campus apartment, grateful to find it empty, which meant her roommate, Brooke, was at her morning class. Tatum's next class wasn't until later that afternoon, but she doubted if she would attend. As she told Coach Mulgrew, her mind was all over the place. She felt so out of sorts, finding herself possibly single and kicked off the cheer team all within a week's time. Tatum realized much of her identity was wrapped up in being a Bruins cheerleader and King's girlfriend. Now that it had all been stripped away, she felt lost.

Tatum strode to the fridge and poured a glass of orange juice, gulping it down and then going to the sink to rinse out the glass. As she held the glass under the flowing water, it slipped from her grasp and shattered, shards of glass nicking her wrist. *Oh, the irony,* Tatum thought, cursing under her breath. Tatum tried to clean up the glass from the sink, slightly cutting her fingers in the process.

When Brooke returned from her class, she found Tatum bandaging her wrist.

Brooke winced. "Ooh. What happened?"

"I cut my wrist," Tatum said, not in the mood for being bothered, but she was careful not to take her sour mood out on Brooke.

Brooke looked at her, her face masked in concern. "So, what did Mr. Keller want?"

"They kicked me off the cheer team."

Brooke's mouth dropped open in disbelief. "You're kidding. Wow. That's so unfair."

"Tell me about it."

"You should protest. Tell them Black Lives Matter."

Tatum rolled her eyes. "Not funny, Brooke."

"I know. I'm sorry. Just trying to cheer you up. Hey, I'm gonna nap before my afternoon class. I'm here if you need anything."

Tatum was tired of the pity from everyone. Sighing, she stood and went into her room and lay across her bed, thinking about tomorrow's victory parade. All classes had been canceled so everyone could attend, but she'd probably just watch on television. It would be too painful to watch the Bruins players and cheerleaders celebrate, knowing she was no longer a part of it all. With these thoughts, Tatum nodded off, and she spent the better part of the day sleeping to escape the nightmare and uncertainty of her new reality.

***

Back in College Station, Jocelyn awakened Gya the following morning, alerting her that she was a trending topic on Twitter.

"Wow. So the interview has already been posted?" Gya sat up and grabbed her phone, her face shining with excitement. But she wasn't prepared for the comments.

So because I'm not a virgin I'm not worthy of being wifed up in the future? Little Miss Polly Purity can have a stadium of seats! (Pun intended)

This is exactly why I don't go to church. Can't stand these pit bulls of the gospel who think they're better than everybody else. Gya is nothing but a jerk for Jesus. Bryant is making a huge mistake if he goes through with the wedding. She is so annoying.

The only thing I took away from this pathetic interview is that Goody-goody Gya will have no idea of how to please Bryant in bed. He needs to call me as soon as he signs that contract, and I'll show him. LOL!

Gya looked at Jocelyn, her eyes wide with hurt and confusion. "Why are people being so ugly and hateful?"

"From what I gathered, you made it seem as if you and Bryant are the perfect couple because of abstinence and looked down on other people for being sexually active. Did you say that marriages won't be as blessed if couples don't choose to wait?" Jocelyn asked.

"No, I didn't. All I said during the interview is what worked for *our* relationship."

Gya's phone rang, and she saw it was her mother, Pam.

"Good morning, baby. I just watched the interview on YouTube. You and Bryant looked great."

Gya burst into tears, her sobs alarming her mother. "Gya? Baby, what's wrong?"

"Mom, the world hates me," Gya sobbed as Jocelyn did her best to try and console her.

"What?"

"I know you don't have a Twitter account, but you should see some of the cruel hashtags and posts. People are saying I think I'm better than everybody."

"Now Gya, calm down. I've seen nothing but positive things on my end. Your interview is being shared on Facebook by numerous Christian groups. Those are the only opinions you need to concern yourself with. It sounds like those naysayers are just jealous, and I told you from the moment you first started dating Bryant that you would have to develop a thicker skin."

"But why do people have to be so mean? I'm only trying to share the love of Christ."

"Gya, dry up those tears, and pay those idiots no mind. Also, this is a lesson about how the media can twist your words. How do we know that the interviewer didn't put her own spin on the things you said to try and fuel controversy?"

After gathering her bearings and assuring her mother she would be alright, Gya hung up, and she and Jocelyn watched the YouTube interview together. Gya had to admit that Toshina hadn't manipulated anything as her mother suggested. And if Gya was totally honest with herself, she could understand how people felt she was coming off preachy and judgmental, even though that wasn't her intent. Going forward, she had to be mindful of measuring her words more carefully. She could already tell that life within the public eye wasn't going to be easy.

"Listen, girl, try not to let this stuff get to you. You shouldn't have to dim your light because it's shining so brightly upon others' insecurities. I remember how Russell and Ciara Wilson experienced backlash when they stated they were practicing abstinence before marriage. And what about Ayesha Curry? Her and Steph came under fire for 'touting' their Christian beliefs. It's sad how we're living in times that glorify wickedness, meanwhile people seeking to live upright are bashed and ridiculed."

"Preach, sis," Gya said with a laugh.

"Glad I made you smile." Jocelyn laughed along with her. "But...I hate to be the bearer of more bad news."

Gya's heart sank again. "What is it now?"

"Some gossip sites are reporting that Tatum tried to commit suicide yesterday."

"What?" Gya shrieked.

"I don't know if it's true or not, but I wanted you to hear it from me first before getting online today. I read that UCLA kicked her out of school for her scene at that nightclub, and King dumped her. Apparently, all of this sent her over the edge, and she tried to slit her wrists."

Gya was shaking her head. "My cousin is strong, and I know she wouldn't go out like that. Look, I'm about to call her."

Jocelyn retreated to give her some privacy, and Gya phoned Tatum who answered on the first ring.

"Tay, are you okay? You didn't try to kill yourself, did you?"

"Gya, I'm fine, but I'm gonna kill Brooke. I know she's the one who started that crazy rumor about me trying to kill myself. I can't believe she'd do something like this to me. I went to her room to confront her, but she must've already gone downtown for the victory parade."

Tatum then filled Gya in on accidently dropping the glass in the sink and nicking her wrist in the process. She also talked about the discussion that took place in Mr. Keller's office.

"Oh, no cousin. Well, you know my motto: Keep your head up, and keep the faith. You might not understand now, but I know God's hands are all over this, and He's going to work everything out for your good."

"I can say the same to you. I read all the garbage that's being written online about you and Bryant. Is this trash Gya and Tatum week or what?" Tatum said, trying to muster a laugh.

Gya laughed along with her. "We come from a strong line of women, so we might be knocked down, but we know how to get right back up and wipe the dust off, don't we?"

"Yes. I know we'll get through this."

"Hey, this is Bryant beeping in. I gotta run but call me if you need anything. Love you, cousin," Gya said.

"Love you more," Tatum said before hanging up.

The sound of Bryant's deep voice soothed Gya's rattled nerves.

"Hey, bae. Just checking on you. I already saw the brutal stuff posted online. I love you, Gya, and I don't care about any of that negativity. You're going to be my wife, and nothing else matters."

Gya's heart melted. "*Awww*. I love you, too, Bryant. How about we meet for breakfast before class?"

"On my way, baby. Love you, girl."

"I love you more."

Chapter Four

Tatum watched the victory parade on television, and after it concluded, she'd dozed off on the sofa. She was awakened by a loud pounding at the front door and the sound of King's voice calling her name. Tatum sat up, disoriented, and thinking she was dreaming, but when he called her name again, she shot up and went to the front door. King stood on the other side; the depths of his brown eyes filled with worry.

"Tay, are you alright?"

Tatum blinked the sleep from her eyes. "Yeah, I'm fine."

"I just heard what happened. Tatum, baby, I'm so sorry. I didn't mean to send you over the edge like that," King said, stepping inside and gently leading her over to the sofa. He placed her head upon his shoulder and kissed her forehead.

While his affection was nice, Tatum didn't want to play the damsel in distress and decided to set the record straight. "King, I didn't try to commit suicide. It was all a rumor started by Brooke. I accidentally dropped a glass yesterday, and it cut my wrist and hands. That's all there is to it."

"So, you weren't kicked out of school? When I didn't see you at the parade today, I knew something was up, but I didn't know what was going on."

"Being kicked out of school was another dumb rumor. But Mr. Keller did remove me from the cheer team due to what happened at The Rooftop."

King sighed. "Man, I feel like this is all my fault. I'm so sorry, Tay."

"It's not, King."

"Look, I know I acted like a total jerk, but Tatum, I want you to know that what we have is for keeps. Wherever I'm drafted, I want you right there by my side."

Tatum hugged him tightly. "And there's nowhere else I'd rather be."

They were interrupted by Brooke entering the apartment. She took one look at the rage that crossed Tatum's face upon seeing her and immediately threw her hands up in defense, her ivory skin growing red as a ripe strawberry.

"Tatum, please hear me out: I told Jason that you cut your wrist, but I never said it was a suicide attempt. All I mentioned is that you were upset about being kicked off the cheer team, and I assume he went and told someone else, and that's how the crazy rumors got started. I'm so sorry. I didn't mean for things to spiral out of control like this."

Tatum was still glaring, being careful to measure her words before speaking. "Brooke, I would kindly appreciate it if you kept my name out of your mouth from this day forward. Don't discuss anything about me with your boyfriend or anyone else. Am I clear?"

Brooke had now gone pale at the venom she heard dripping from her roommate's voice. She meekly nodded and tossed King a sheepish look of apology before slinking to her bedroom.

King whistled and laughed. "I can tell the final few months of the semester are gonna be pretty tense in here."

"Not if she stays out of my way. Brooke runs her mouth too much. That's always been her problem." Tatum could feel her anger waning a bit. She was just glad to have her man back. She began to reason that following King away from UCLA was for the best. She couldn't wait to see what the future held for the next chapter of their relationship.

***

"...the Miami Waves select Bryant Green, running back, Texas A&M."

It was a Saturday afternoon in mid-April, and the voice of NFL Commissioner Roger Goodell was nearly drowned out by the deafening applause of the audience. The NFL draft had returned to New York City's Radio Music Hall. Bryant, Gya, and his family were seated in a backstage reception area of the venue. His mother, Yolanda, pulled him in for a huge hug and a kiss, followed by his father, Bryce, dapping him up. His older sister, Shanna, was a bundle of tears as she hugged and kissed him before passing her brother off to Gya who was overflowing with emotion for her fiancé as well. She couldn't have been prouder of Bryant.

Bryant received more thunderous applause as he took the stage and was presented with the Waves black-and-aqua-blue team jersey and matching hat. Placing the hat upon his head and hoisting his new jersey in the air, he posed for the flashing cameras with Mr. Goodell. Pretty soon, Bryant was posing for photos with Gya and the rest of his family. Gya beamed, her heart full of joy for her man and glad the craziness of the *I Said Yes* interview was behind them.

Just as her mother said, the world was soon fixated on the next juicy story and had moved on. Gya was determined to do the same.

After leaving Radio City Music Hall, everyone decided to have dinner at Tavern on the Green. Gya got a taste of what being married to a high-profile athlete would entail, as they could barely get through their meal due to all of the strangers approaching their table to give Bryant congratulatory greetings and well wishes.

"You know, son, we're going to have to keep you prayed up. You always remember the values your mother and I instilled in you and keep that good head on your shoulders. Don't get caught up in anything stupid. It's hard for blacks to get a second chance after screwing up," Bryant's father, Bryce, said.

"You know I'll stay prayed up for my baby." Bryce's mother reached over to rub Bryant's back.

"And he'll have a wife who's praying just as hard," Gya assured with a smile.

After leaving the restaurant, they returned to their hotel, the Marriott Marquis in Times Square. Gya was astonished to discover that Bryant had plans to hang out later that evening with a few of the Waves players, one of whom was Jamison Grant, a player who was known for being a notorious playboy.

"Bryant, are you sure that's a good idea?" Gya asked with a frown. "I've heard all about Jamison's reputation, and I'd hate for him to get you wrapped up in some foolishness. You need to steer clear of him."

"He's my teammate now, Gya, so that will be a bit hard to do," Bryant said, and Gya detected a slight edge in his voice.

"Are you really going to hang out at a club? Bryant, you need to be careful. I mean your dad just had this discussion with you at the restaurant. It's not good for your image to be seen at some nightspot."

"Gya, won't you just back off, okay? If my mother isn't nagging me about it, then what's your problem?" Bryant finally exploded.

Gya's eyes widened in shock at his harsh tone. "Wow. Okay then. Fine. Guess I'll see you later."

Sighing, Bryant started to speak and then decided it was best to just leave her hotel room. Without another word, he closed the door softly behind him, leaving Gya to stand dumbfounded and ponder what exactly just happened. Was Bryant already starting to change for the worse right before her eyes?

Gya mindlessly flipped through channels on the television. She glanced at her phone, and the time was three minutes past eleven-thirty. Her fingers had been itching all night to text Bryant and ask how everything was going, but she didn't want to upset him further by trying to keep tabs on him. Not to mention she was still so infuriated at the attitude he'd displayed earlier. Gya had never been the jealous type, and she didn't like the insecurity that she felt creeping in. Sighing, she decided to get up and shower. She drifted off to sleep after midnight and was awakened by a knock at her door.

Glancing at the bedside clock, she saw that it was 2:42 a.m. She got up and walked to the door, rubbing at her eyes. She found Bryant standing on the other side.

"Hi, baby. Sorry to wake you...*ummm*...Can I come in?"

Gya stepped aside and allowed him entry without a word.

They stood in the middle of the room in an awkward silence. Finally, Bryant exhaled and rubbed his hand across his face. "I'm sorry, Gya. I promise I could hardly enjoy myself tonight because all I could think about was how I hurt you. I behaved like a total jerk, and you know that's totally out of character for me."

Gya was moved by the sincerity in his voice. "Apology accepted."

Bryant pulled her into his warm embrace, and they hugged tightly for a good minute, neither wanting to be the first to let go.

"To be honest, my father's words at dinner really got to me. I know the challenges black players face. Shoot, I've felt it all throughout my years at Texas A&M. Coach wasn't comfortable starting me until my junior year. That's why I always gave it my all every time I stepped out into the field. Honestly, there were times where I didn't even think I stood a chance of being drafted because I felt I wasn't being given a fair chance to display my talent."

"Well, we see that God had the final say right? Remember Proverbs eighteen and sixteen? A man's gift makes room for him and brings him before great men. I promise you, baby, God is not finished with you yet. The best is yet to come," Gya encouraged.

Bryant kissed her long and hard. "I love you so much, girl. What did I ever do to deserve you?"

"I'm just as blessed to have you. So how did it go tonight? How many groupies had to be peeled off you and the rest of your future teammates?" Gya asked, only half kidding.

Bryant laughed. "It wasn't even like that. We just chilled at this lounge, and I got to know a few of the players. Yeah, there were a lot of females lurking around, but it's nothing I've never encountered before. Baby, trust me, you have nothing to worry about. You're my one and only."

"And you'd better not ever forget that," Gya said, playfully punching his arm.

They shared a goodnight kiss before he left to get some sleep. Gya was thankful they were able to put the ugly argument behind them. She couldn't wait for them to start building their new future together. She went to sleep with her lips still tingling from his soothing kiss.

Chapter Five

The month of May was a whirlwind of activity, marked by Tatum preparing to say goodbye to UCLA. She was more confident about leaving college and joining King on his journey into the NBA.

Meanwhile Gya and Bryant walked across the stage to receive their degrees and were official college graduates. Gya's parents hosted an extravagant joint graduation party for the couple, not long after which Bryant and Gya traveled to Miami to house hunt. His five-year contract worth forty million dollars—in addition to the twenty-five-million-dollar signing bonus—blessed them with the opportunity to search within the city of Miami's most exclusive neighborhoods. They'd narrowed their options between the Coconut Grove community where many Waves and Miami Heat players were residents and Hibiscus Island. Gya wanted a view of the Biscayne Bay from her backyard. But the realtor informed them that their preferred neighborhood of Camp Biscayne was so exclusive that homes were rarely for sale. Fortunately, Gya fell in love with a five-bedroom Spanish-style home in the gated community of Hibiscus Island. It also housed a separate villa their parents could stay in whenever they visited. Seeing that his future bride was pleased, Bryant placed an offer on the home, and soon they were whisked off to sign the paperwork to close the deal.

Now new homeowners, Bryant and Gya decided to explore the sights and attractions of their new city. Hand in hand, they walked along the streets of Coconut Grove, taking in the sidewalk cafes, and eventually touring the CocoWalk mall. They were interrupted repeatedly by autograph and photo op seekers. Gya browsed through the chic clothing boutiques while Bryant interacted with the fans welcoming him to their city. Again, she got a taste of what she was in for as Bryant's wife. While she found it intrusive, she understood it came with the territory and remembered she was pledging a lifetime of for better or for worse.

Bryant and Gya ended their tour of Miami with a beachside stroll against the illustrious waters of South Beach while nibbling on churros and periodically waving at awestruck beachgoers snapping photos of them.

"Thanks for being such a good sport today with all the fans, bae. I know it can be a bit overwhelming," Bryant said as if reading her earlier thoughts.

"No thanks necessary. Thank you for blessing me with a beautiful new home."

Bryant stopped and gazed deep into her eyes. "I want to spend the rest of my life making you happy, Gya."

"You already know it's not about the material things. I'd be just as happy if you were using your degree to work in corporate, Bryant."

"Oh, trust me, I know. That's why I love you so much."

"Ditto," Gya said, using a line borrowed from one of her favorite movies, *Ghost*. Finishing her churro, she bent and flicked sand at Bryant.

Bryant laughed. "That's how you gonna do me after I declare my love? See, I'm about to pick you up and throw you into that water."

"Bryant, you'd better not," Gya screeched, taking off running.

Bryant took off after her and swooped her up.

"Bryant, stop. I'm not playing. You'd better not put me in that water."

Instead, Bryant planted a long, deep kiss on her lips, a kiss Gya eagerly returned against the backdrop of the beach and setting Miami sun.

***

The Saturday of the much-anticipated nuptials of Gya Lawson and Bryant Green had finally arrived. The ceremony was taking place at Genesis Tabernacle, a church Gya and her family had been members of since she was an infant. Tatum and the rest of the women in Gya's bridal party, which consisted of Tatum, her roommate Jocelyn, Bryant's older sister Shanna, and Gya's cousin Jasmin, were waiting in a conference room of the church. The ladies had a chance to become better acquainted at Gya's bridal shower brunch, which was held at Brenner's on the Bayou, an upscale steak restaurant. This gathering was the extent of Gya's bachelorette festivities as she didn't want a wild and raucous shindig with male strippers, which Tatum teasingly suggested. Their cousin Jasmin was a bit miffed that Gya had selected Tatum as her maid of honor. Tatum reasoned that had Jasmin been married by now instead of being so focused on medical school, she could at least have been appointed as matron of honor.

Tatum was genuinely happy for Gya and Bryant, but this wedding would also serve as a family reunion of sorts, and she knew she would come in contact with her father and his wife, Genevieve. Like always, their exchange of pleasantries would feel so forced and awkward. This honestly summed up her interaction with her paternal side of the family, a line of prominent doctors. As a matter of fact, they had been disappointed when Gya's mother, Pam, chose not to pursue a career as a physician. She married a doctor instead.

The Addison family reputation suffered another stain when they learned of Vanessa's pregnancy with Tatum. Tatum's parents crossed paths at a hospital in the late nineties where Charles was a practicing surgeon and Vanessa was a nurse. They engaged in clandestine flings within the hospital's on-call rooms between shifts, which resulted in the unplanned pregnancy. But to the chagrin of his parents, as well as Vanessa, Charles refused to rectify the situation by placing a ring on the finger of a woman he deemed as being beneath him.

Now the Addison family was looking to Jasmin to carry on the medical torch since Gya nor Tatum had any plans to pursue medical school or so much as a degree within the medical field. Jasmin was the daughter of the eldest sister, Angela, a pediatrician.

Now Tatum stood poised in her purple chiffon one-shoulder gown with a side slit that showed off her long, svelte leg. Tatum had loved the strapless design of the same gown, but it was typical of Gya to insist that all in her bridal party display modesty. The ladies sat and chitchatted while waiting for Gya. Last report, Gya had just finishing having her makeup done and was in the process of sliding into her dress, after which a limousine would transport her to the church.

***

"Ready, princess?" Gya's father, Dr. Matthew Lawson, asked as he helped his daughter out of the limo and extended his arm for her to take as he prepared to escort her down the aisle.

Gya smiled and nodded, already on the verge of tears as the realization of marrying her soulmate sank in. Gya was demure in a white beaded lace trumpet-style gown with tank sleeves that showcased her smooth and toned arms. A sheer chapel train adorned her head, and it flowed behind her in the light June breeze of Houston as she strode toward the entrance of the church where her groom waited.

Gya floated down the aisle to the beautiful melody of Kurt Carr's "I Believe God," her eyes never losing contact with Bryant's. She thought she'd lose her composure as she witnessed his own eyes glisten with tears as he took in the breathtaking sight of his bride. She and Bryant had written their own personal vows to share with each other, which was followed by the sand ceremony as a soloist belted out a soul-stirring rendition of "The Lord's Prayer." The congregation erupted with applause when the minister pronounced them husband and wife, and Bryant and Gya sealed their union with a kiss, neither wanting to be the first to break away.

Chapter Six

After posing for professional photos at the church, the bride, groom, and their wedding party were whisked away in limousines to The Post Oak Hotel in Uptown Houston for the elegant reception hosted in the grand ballroom. Cocktail hour was in full swing when they arrived, and Tatum eagerly grabbed a flute of champagne from the tray of a tuxedoed waiter. She was beyond impressed, as her aunt and uncle had spared no expense for their baby girl's wedding day. After the official introduction of Mr. and Mrs. Bryant Green and their wedding party, Gya and Bryant shared their first dance to John Legend's "All of Me."

Tatum sat with King as she took in her cousin and her new husband swaying and gazing deeply into each other's eyes. It was a beautiful song, and as Tatum listened to the lyrics, she realized John's words summed up her relationship with King almost perfectly. Feeling her eyes well with tears, Tatum clasped King's hand, gripping it tightly as she resolved to remain at his side for the long run. After all, that's what true love was about.

Gya and her father then danced to Levert's rendition of "Wind Beneath My Wings," followed by Bryant and his mother taking the floor to Boyz II Men's "A Song for Mama."

Tatum went to the ladies' room to freshen up her makeup before dinner was served. She found her aunt Angela and Jasmin standing near the sinks, and Tatum guessed they had the same idea.

"Isn't Gya the most gorgeous bride you've ever seen?" Angela cooed. "I am so proud of her. I've told all my employees and patients about my niece who saved herself for her wedding day. I promise you she's about the only twenty-something I know that can wear white."

Tatum had to refrain from rolling her eyes.

"You don't have to rub it in, Mother," Jasmin said, giving her mom a mock chastising look.

"Baby, you know I'm just as proud of you, my future obstetrician," Angela said. Then she cut her eyes at Tatum. "Tatum, I'm going to have to be honest; I was very embarrassed about your behavior when I saw that video. You really need to learn to get that temper under control, but I know you can't help it.

I remember how Vanessa used to make Charles' life a living hell when she was chasing him down back in the day."

"Aunt Angela, the only thing my mom chased my father down about is getting him to have a true relationship with *me*," Tatum asserted.

Angela smirked. "Oh, so that's the narrative your mom spun to you?"

"I heard you plan to follow King to wherever he's drafted. If I were you, I'd be front and center for Gya's bouquet toss later. You're gonna need it," Jasmin interjected.

"So, you and King plan to cohabitate? Well, it's your life, niecey, but please don't go getting knocked up. You see how that worked out with your mother and father," Angela said.

"Trust me, I'm fine. And actually, I'll leave space for both you and Jasmin during the bridal toss. Since I already have a man, you *single* ladies need to catch that bouquet more than I do, don't you think?" Tatum said.

She knew it was catty, but she couldn't help getting a dig in, especially since her aunt Angela had been single for years since Jasmin's father left her for another woman. And Tatum couldn't blame him. She didn't understand how any man could deal with her pretentious and overbearing aunt. Both Jasmin and Angela were dumbfounded into silence and glared at Tatum as she reapplied her lipstick, gave them a wave goodbye, and sashayed out of the restroom.

Back inside of the ballroom, guests dined on red snapper with crawfish cream sauce, broiled main lobster tail, and steamed vegetables. Despite her run-in with her cousin and aunt, Tatum was determined to enjoy the rest of the evening. Her father, Charles, surprised her after dinner by extending his hand and asking her to dance.

"You look beautiful tonight, Tatum," Charles said as they spun to Natalie Cole's rendition of "Unforgettable" along with the other guests. "Where's Vanessa?"

"She had to work," Tatum said quickly, which was the truth, although Gya had extended an invite. But her mother didn't want to see Charles and Genevieve.

"Oh, well, tell her I said hello," Charles said.

As the song concluded, he kissed her cheek and returned to sit with his wife. Tatum's heart was full, and she hoped this marked the beginning of them embarking on a closer relationship.

***

Gya, ever gracious, made a point of making her way around the ballroom and greeting each guest, thanking them for taking part in her special day. The bouquet and garter toss commenced, followed by more dancing and fun. Before Gya and Bryant realized it, it was well past midnight, and the reception began to wind to a close.

Tatum hugged Gya goodbye.

"I still can't believe my big cuz is a married woman now. So happy for you and Bryant both. Now go upstairs and rock his world tonight, girl."

Gya blushed and playfully slapped Tatum on her shoulder. "I done told you about being in my bedroom."

"Call me tomorrow with all the details," Tatum said.

"Girl, bye. I'm not sharing my husband's bedroom skills with you or anyone else. Besides, we're gonna be preparing to leave for Paris tomorrow."

"Enjoy your weeklong honeymoon, cousin. Love you," Tatum said, kissing her cousin on the cheek.

Gya reconnected with Bryant in the lobby of the hotel, as he returned from walking his parents out to the valet to retrieve their vehicle.

"Did I tell you how beautiful you looked today, Mrs. Green?" Bryant said, taking in his new bride as he strode toward her.

"Yes, but I'll never get tired of hearing you say it," Gya replied as he took her by the hand and escorted her toward the elevator bank. They'd reserved the presidential suite for their first night as husband and wife. Once reaching their quarters, Gya giggled as Bryant carried her over the threshold. Placing Gya down upon the massive king-sized bed, Bryant gazed into the depths of her eyes. He then engulfed her lips with his own.

Gya's heartbeat accelerated from both excitement and desire. As she returned Bryant's kisses, she was filled with exhilaration at knowing this time neither would have to practice self-control and pull away. She moaned in pleasure as Bryant practically ripped her dress from her body. Without shame or abandon of trying to be a prim and proper lady, she tore at his clothing as well. Nearly dizzy with anticipation, Gya clamped her legs around Bryant's waist as he entered her for the first time. A tiny gasp of discomfort escaped her lips, and her manicured nails dug into his back. A sheen of tears welled within her eyes as the moment of pain turned into immense pleasure—a pleasure she didn't ever want to end. Time was suspended for Gya, and her euphoria intensified when Bryant released a throaty, guttural groan as he neared his apex of satisfaction. Soon, Gya lost control and uttered a cry of ecstasy as she reached her own peak.

Bryant collapsed on top of his wife, squeezing her smooth and soft skin tightly as he tried to catch his breath and gather his bearings. Gya stroked his back as Bryant kissed her upon her forehead, which was damp with perspiration, as they basked in the afterglow of their lovemaking.

After gathering their bearings, Bryant scooped his wife into his arms once again and carried her into the lavish bathroom where he turned on the showerhead. Passion re-consumed them as they washed each other's bodies under the flow of water. They soon returned to the bed and proceeded to make love again well into the wee hours of the next morning.

Chapter Seven

The crowd of the Barclays Center roared with approval as King was announced as the number one, first round draft pick for their home team, the New York City Flash.

Tatum clapped just as hard as she and his family watched from the seating area as King took the stage and posed with NBA Commissioner Adam Silver, holding the orange-and-black Flash jersey bearing his last name and number.

The next few days were a flash for Tatum as she hardly saw King. While he was being formally introduced to the city of New York at a team press conference, Tatum went house hunting with her mother, Vanessa, and King's mother, Michelle. King signed a four-year contract worth fifty million dollars, and with that in mind, Tatum decided on a three-bedroom apartment in Central Park South. She liked the fact there was only one other apartment on the entire floor, not to mention the beautiful view of Central Park from their living room. The apartment was fifty thousand dollars a month, and King didn't even blink at the amount when she phoned him with the details. He encouraged her to make an offer, trusting her judgment. He ended the call promising to catch up with her later at their hotel. Not yet ready to call it a day, Tatum suggested to Vanessa and Michelle that they go somewhere to have lunch. They decided on a quaint restaurant in Soho.

"Michelle, you must be so proud of King. I can't wait to see him crush the NBA," Vanessa said as they boarded a subway.

"I am very proud. But honestly this moment is so bittersweet. I wish my Korey were here to take part in it all. It's hard to celebrate when you know your house is divided. King and Jacoby's relationship with Korey has been strained ever since he decided to stop hiding his truth and be open about his homosexuality."

"I can imagine how difficult that must be," Vanessa soothed.

"Well, you tell my future brother-in-law that I still love him," Tatum encouraged.

She knew King felt that Korey's being gay somehow brought his own sexuality into question, which she thought was ridiculous. She felt bad for Korey, having his own brother and father be ashamed of him.

"I just don't want King's fame to drive a wedge in our family. I've read horror stories of how some athletes or other celebrities become estranged from their family members. No money in the world is worth me losing my relationship with my sons," Michelle continued.

"Well, I think it's good that King has hired his father as his manager," Vanessa said.

Michelle rolled her eyes. "Jacoby says he's King's public image consultant," she said, making air quotes with her fingers.

The ladies shared a laugh, which lightened the mood again.

"Tatum, I'm sure you'll be busy with getting the apartment in order while King is participating in the NBA Summer League program. I'm glad he has you here to look after things. Of course, I'll always be available to assist should you need me," Michelle assured.

Tatum smiled and nodded, as that's what she'd always loved about Mrs. Michelle. She never overstepped her boundaries and interfered with her relationship with King. Tatum read stories of how some pro athlete moms were so overbearing and selfish, wanting their son's money and fame all to themselves. She found it a blessing that she didn't have to deal with such.

***

Once returning from their weeklong honeymoon in Paris, Bryant and Gya settled into their new lives in Miami. Gya researched different churches, and she and Bryant visited a Sunday service at the First Baptist Church of Coral Gables. Gya felt welcomed from the moment she walked in and enjoyed the service as well as the Word delivered. She and Bryant decided to visit a few more services before making a commitment to join.

The Waves hosted a team mixer aboard a yacht, an all-white attire party where Gya had an opportunity to meet the rest of the Waves organization along with their spouses and significant others. A beautiful woman named Christal approached Gya, introducing herself as the wife of Waves tight end Victor Moore. Christal was of African American and Puerto Rican heritage. Friendly and bubbly, she took Gya under her wing, introducing her to the other wives and girlfriends. They all chatted and got acquainted on the deck of the yacht.

"So, Gya, tell us all about your wedding night and getting that cherry popped for the first time," a woman named Marsai boldly inquired.

Gya was stunned at her audaciousness. Why couldn't people stay out of her and Bryant's bedroom? It was as if her past virginal state made her an anomaly to speculate over, and she didn't like or appreciate it. Fortunately, Christal came to her rescue.

"Marsai, get you some business. Gya, why don't you tell us about your honeymoon in Paris?" Christal encouraged.

A girlfriend of a Waves wide receiver pretended to yawn. "You know how many times Anthony and I have gone to Paris?"

"Well, I'm interested in hearing how she enjoyed it," Christal insisted.

"Paris is just as beautiful as I imagined. It was my first time visiting and I can't wait to return." Gya said.

"Wow, so many 'firsts' for you, Gya. Seems like you've grown up so sheltered. Typical of a Texan," Marsai said.

Gya's frown deepened, and she decided she didn't like this Marsai woman. Since she was merely the girlfriend of an offensive lineman, Gya wondered if she would soon be replaced. She then chided herself for such ugly thoughts.

The remainder of the mixer went by with no further catty remarks, and Gya marveled at the spread of the seafood buffet. It was obvious the Waves organization believed in partying in style and spared no expense.

"Do the ladies attend church together? Do you guys hold weekly Bible studies?" Gya asked Christal once they were alone.

Christal smirked at Gya as she took a sip of champagne. "*Ummm*...no. Honestly, I'm not very religious. Not that I don't believe in God. It's just...well, my family are practicing Catholics."

"Oh, well, that's okay. No judgment here. You think the ladies would be interested in starting a weekly Bible study? I could even lead and host it from my home. I conducted Bible studies at Texas A&M. I think it's important to keep our men covered in prayer whenever they travel and step out on the field."

Christal shrugged, clearly uninterested. "I mean, I dunno. You could give it a shot, I guess."

The following day as Gya was unpacking the last few boxes from their move, she came upon her wedding dress. Smiling, she pressed the dress against her chest in remembrance of that beautiful and blessed day. The wedding video had been uploaded to her YouTube page, and it had over a million views.

Gya was suddenly struck with an idea. There was a fire down in her to do something big for God and have her voice heard throughout the nations. What if she transformed people's fascination with purity into something worthwhile? A type of mentoring program of sorts? She was driven by the notion to encourage women to hold tightly to their virginity and wait for God to bless them with husbands, just as she did. Gya's heart leaped with excitement as she realized now was the time to take Well Worth the Wait global as she'd dreamed.

Chapter Eight

An afternoon shortly after the Fourth of July holiday found Tatum alone in the apartment, bored. She'd spent the better part of the day watching hair and makeup tutorial videos on YouTube. King and the Flash were in Las Vegas to participate in the NBA Summer League games. Now Gya's voice droned in the background from an Instagram live video. As of late, Gya had been going live on social media daily with motivational videos geared toward purity. Both Tatum and her mother, Vanessa, had chuckled about it, with Vanessa dubbing Gya a pseudo-preacher. Gya's videos brought in thousands of followers, and Vanessa surmised that given Gya was married to Bryant, the followers were merely tuning in because she was his wife.

"Take note, Tatum," Vanessa advised. "Gya is too prideful to realize it, but she's building her brand upon Bryant's name. I doubt people would be interested in listening to her holy ramblings otherwise. Not to mention a lot of people are curious given her slip-up a few months back with that purity garbage. Remember, you can always turn controversy into something positive. She managed to turn skeptics and naysayers into an audience."

Tatum was interrupted from her wandering thoughts by the sound of the apartment intercom buzzer, which signaled a guest. She frowned as she walked over to the intercom, as she wasn't expecting anyone.

"Yes, Dominic?" Tatum addressed the concierge of the apartment building through the speaker.

"Good afternoon, Ms. Addison. Mrs. Kelsea West and Mrs. Ariana Parker are here in the lobby. Am I clear to send them up?"

Tatum paused, recognizing Kelsea and Ariana as the wives of two Flash players, Russell and Antoine. They'd never formally met, so why were they here? Her heart sank. Did something happen to King?

"Yes, yes. Please allow them upstairs. Thank you, Dominic."

When Kelsea and Ariana arrived at her front door minutes later, giggling and chattering, Tatum's fears were put at ease.

"Hello, Tatum. Sorry to show up unannounced, but King asked us to keep you company while he and the team are in Vegas," Kelsea said.

Kelsea was an elegant and statuesque chocolate-skinned beauty who looked as if she could've done a stint in the WNBA with her long and shapely legs. Tatum recalled King mentioning that Kelsea used to be a ballerina, per the Flash grapevine.

Ariana was just as gorgeous, her smooth olive skin and full pouty lips boasting of her Latina heritage.

"Wow. King really thought I needed babysitters?" Tatum said with a laugh as she allowed the two women inside.

"This place is fantastic," Kelsea exclaimed, her brown eyes sweeping over the apartment in admiration. "Who's your interior decorator?"

"Believe it or not, both our mothers decorated," Tatum replied.

"It's nice," Ariana agreed.

"We've been wanting to meet you, Tatum, and we felt now was as good a time as any with the guys away for the next week or so. How about an afternoon of shopping and some lunch? Then we can have a watch party over at my home for the first summer league game." Kelsea said.

Tatum smiled. "Sounds like a plan. Let me just slide into something more decent."

"Your makeup is fabulous. Did you do it yourself?" Ariana asked.

"Yeah. I was bored and just decided to play around on my face," Tatum said with a laugh.

"It looks awesome. Kels, we must get Tatum to hook our faces up whenever we have special team events and photo shoots," Ariana said.

Tatum offered both ladies something to drink, and they settled on bottles of water, which they sat and drank while Tatum disappeared into her room to change into a floral-print Dolce & Gabbana sundress. When Tatum returned fully dressed with a D&G clutch purse in hand, she secured the apartment, and they headed to Fifth Avenue in a chauffeured vehicle Kelsea had reserved for the afternoon.

Tatum couldn't help but feel as if she were in a dream as they ventured into stores like Tiffany & Co., Louis Vuitton, Gucci, and Prada. Kelsea nor Ariana flinched at the price tags of the garments and purses they selected. Tatum had King's credit card on hand, and she was a bit hesitant to make hefty purchases, but she eventually loosened up and found her hands loaded with shopping bags. She couldn't believe this was her life now. From a cheerleading scholarship student to someone who could purchase a designer dress from Bergdorf Goodman.

The ladies also made a trip to Sephora, and Tatum felt like she was in heaven. She helped both Kelsea and Ariana shop for different makeup combinations, promising to show them some application techniques. Now a bit exhausted, but famished, the three new friends ended their shopping excursion with lunch at Nobu.

After lunch, the chauffer dropped Tatum back at her apartment with Kelsea promising to send the vehicle to pick her up and transport her to Kelsea's home in New Jersey to watch the game. All agreed that they need a quick nap after such a busy afternoon.

Tatum strode inside the silent apartment, glad that she now had Ariana and Kelsea to hang out with whenever King was away. The apartment had been quite lonely and silent without King's presence. Before departing for Vegas, King had spent most of his time lounging around the apartment playing video games in between weightlifting and conditioning at the Flash team facility. He also had several business meetings with his father and agent. And of course, he and Tatum spent a lot of time making love now that they were cohabitating.

Tatum would never admit this to Gya, but she was starting to feel convicted about living with King without a ring. She didn't want King to grow comfortable with their living arrangement and not feel the need to propose. She recalled how she'd initiated talk about their future a few days prior to his departure. King revealed he wanted four children and made it clear he expected Tatum to be a stay-at-home mom. Tatum mulled this was why King wasn't too enthusiastic about her finishing her degree online at NYU.

"Bae, I practically became a multi-millionaire overnight. There's nothing that a college degree can afford you that I can't. Let's just focus on building our family."

"We're not building anything with this ring finger bare, King," Tatum pointed out.

King had chuckled. "All in due time, baby doll."

King also discussed setting boundaries with their families, citing his annoyance with Tatum always being on the phone with her mother.

"Tay, when I arrive home from practices and games, I want your undivided attention." King then surprised her with a moment of transparency. He revealed he was already feeling out of place as an incoming NBA rookie. Students at UCLA had treated him like a god, but here in New York, he felt like a small fish in a big pond and felt the pressure of living up to his multi-million-dollar contract. Otherwise, the people of New York, along with his teammates, would have his head if he didn't measure up.

Tatum assured King she would have his back every step of the way and tried to limit her talking time with Vanessa, at least while King was present at home. She didn't want to do anything to add to his stress level or mounting sense of pressure. Tatum would show King he had nothing to worry about as far as their relationship was concerned. With their family living in different states, Tatum was the only support system he had, and she resolved to be the strongest backbone possible for her man.

Chapter Nine

"Surprise!"

Gya clasped her hands to her mouth in astonishment upon walking into a private room of her new favorite restaurant, Cipriani Downtown Miami, and seeing her family along with Christal, her husband, and a few of Bryant's other teammates standing and cheering. It was Gya's twenty-third birthday, and Bryant had reserved the restaurant's exclusive Venetian Room. What she thought would be a romantic dinner between the two of them was a surprise birthday party.

Gya turned to Bryant and planted a big, juicy kiss on his lips before going to greet everyone. Even Tatum was present with King, and Gya was touched her cousin had secretly flown in to celebrate with her.

Gya was feeling fabulous. Well Worth the Wait had taken off to heights unknown, and she was blown away by the move of God. Her social media following had skyrocketed, and this compelled Gya to start vlogging. Her weekly YouTube videos consisted of her morning prayer and workout routine, along with meal prep and healthy eating tips. She'd even started hosting live Bible studies each week, streaming simultaneously on Instagram, Facebook, and YouTube. Just the day before, Gya had received her first invite for a speaking engagement. She would be one of the keynote speakers at a women's empowerment conference taking place at ONE Church Los Angeles in the fall. It was one of the best birthday gifts she could've received, and she was excited to see how many more blessings the twenty-third chapter of her life would bring. God had already showed up and showed out, and it was off to a promising start.

Christal introduced Gya to her cousin, a young and shapely Puerto Rican girl named Mercedes.

"I hope you don't mind that I brought her along. She's visiting, and I didn't want to just leave her home alone."

"It's no problem. Nice to meet you, Mercedes, and thank you for coming to celebrate my birthday with me," Gya said, giving her a friendly hug.

"Thanks so much for having me," Mercedes said with a smile.

"Mercedes's thinking about transferring to the University of Miami to complete her studies and is touring the campus while she's here." Christal explained.

"Hopefully, I'll land me a baller like you and Christal." Mercedes laughed.

Gya couldn't help but laugh at the young and impressionable Mercedes and made a point of remembering to pray later that God would lead Mercedes to make the right decision in choosing a school, not one based on such superficial means.

Once the party was in full swing, Gya walked around with her phone, filming footage she'd share on her birthday vlog. Gya also wanted to record date nights with her and Bryant, but her mother Pam was not in agreement, feeling that Gya shouldn't make herself so accessible and keep certain aspects of her life private. Gya respected her mother's opinion, but she wanted her marriage to Bryant to serve as an example to other women that you can be rich, famous, and godly.

"So, when do your online classes at NYU begin?" Gya asked Tatum as they gazed out the panoramic windows at the Biscayne Bay. The waters shimmered beneath the mid-July moon of Miami.

"I'm holding off on that. Moving to NYC was a huge adjustment, and honestly, I'm a bit too distracted right now to focus on school," Tatum replied.

"What? Is this King talking or you?" Gya asked.

"Gya, don't stand here and insult my intelligence. But since you asked, King agrees with me taking a break from school."

Gya glanced over in King's direction. He was engaged in a lively discussion with Bryant and his teammates.

"Tay, can I be honest? I feel King doesn't want you to finish school because he'd be intimidated with you having completed your degree. I don't think he wants you one-upping him."

"Gya, now you're being ridiculous, and for the sake of us being at your birthday party, I will end this conversation and politely ask that you mind your own business," Tatum said. She turned on her heels and went back to join King at their table without a second glance at Gya.

Gya shrugged off her cousin's attitude. Tatum would just have to learn the hard way that she was making a mistake by placing her life on hold for King.

***

After a fabulous birthday celebration, the good news just kept coming for Gya. Claire's, a jewelry and accessory retail company, had accepted her proposal for a sponsorship of a line of purity rings for Well Worth the Wait. The idea had come to Gya to host an annual purity conference and retreat in which young ladies would wear white debutante ball–style dresses and present themselves as brides of Christ, pledging to remain abstinent or celibate until marriage. Gya was so excited because she'd loved Claire's retail since high school, and it was a dream come true to partner with them for her ministry. Gya was hard at work with planning the purity conference, researching venues. She wanted to hold the inaugural conference in her hometown of Houston and was planning it for next summer since most of her followers were college women and they would be on hiatus from school during that time.

While in the middle of outlining her plans for the conference, Bryant phoned. He'd departed for training camp earlier that week, and Gya missed him.

"How's it going there?"

"Man, I thought college two-a-days were brutal. It's nothing compared to the pros," Bryant said, going on to admit to Gya that he was feeling an immense amount of pressure to make the roster and accumulate playing time as a rookie once the season officially started. "They've already made a few cuts. Just trying to secure my spot."

"Babe, you have nothing to worry about. They drafted you for a reason, and you're forgetting that God has you in His hands. And you know I'm praying for you daily. I love you."

"I love you more. Counting the days when I can get back home to you."

They chatted a bit longer, and when Gya hung up, she was smiling widely, feeling so blessed to have such an awesome husband along with a growing and thriving ministry. She couldn't ask God for anything better at that moment.

***

"Who was that at the door?" Vanessa asked on the other end of the phone as Tatum thanked the pharmacy delivery boy, tipped him, and closed the door.

"The pharmacy has just delivered my refill of birth control pills," Tatum responded.

"What? Tatum, you're still taking those things?"

Tatum frowned, although her mom couldn't see her. "Yes, Mom. Why would I stop?"

"Didn't you say King was discussing you two starting a family?"

"After *marriage*, Mom."

"Tatum, a baby will bring that ring to you a lot sooner," Vanessa advised.

"Mom, I am not trapping King into marrying me."

"Better you than someone else. You know how these players are often hit with paternity suits. Now I love King, but I'm well aware he's a full-blooded male. I put nothing past him, and I'd hate for some other groupie chick to bear his child before you. Tatum, listen to your mother: Secure your future *now*."

Tatum couldn't believe her mother's words, and now she realized this was probably the same thing she'd tried to do to Charles, but it backfired on her. No wonder her father's side of the family never had anything good to say about Vanessa.

"So be it, Mom. I refuse to be another baby mama, and I want to have a child with King as my *husband*. And that's final. I don't want to have this discussion with you again."

"Fine. Suit yourself. Let's just hope and pray I'm wrong," Vanessa said. "I need to get ready for my shift. I can't wait until you and King finally do tie the knot because I plan to retire from nursing as soon as you do."

"I don't suggest you do that because I'm telling you right now, Mom, King and I aren't taking care of you."

"Oh really? After I took care of *you* for so many years?"

"I didn't ask to be born, Mom. You did what you had to do as a single mother. That was a choice you made when you got pregnant in an effort to trap my father. He's resented you ever since and resents me by default, which wasn't fair to me. I refuse to place my child in the same position by doing what you did. I truly love King and am no gold digger. I won't allow you to try and mooch off him either."

Vanessa gasped. "Tatum, how dare you talk to me like that."

"It's a truth that's long overdue, Mom. Now goodbye."

Tatum hung up with tears stinging her eyes. Ever since King had gotten drafted into the league, her mother had turned into someone she didn't recognize. Every conversation they had revolved around King and his money, and Tatum was sick of it. She realized she had no problem with cutting her mother off if it came to that. She wouldn't allow Vanessa to take advantage of King and ruin her relationship with him. It was something she was willing to protect at all costs.

Chapter Ten

"Father God, we pray that you keep Bryant covered on this afternoon. May your hedge of protection enshroud him and his fellow Waves teammates as they are out on the field..." Bryant's mother prayed.

Gya stood within a circle consisting of her parents and Bryant's family as they prepared to head to the stadium for the Waves' season opener. Gya was capturing the prayer live via her Instagram feed. Once the prayer had concluded, she glanced at the thousands of comments left by her followers and Bryant's fans, which consisted of "amens" and other encouraging words.

"Gya, you should've been focused on praying with us instead of having cameras in our faces. That prayer was a private family moment," Pam chided her daughter as they prepared to load into vehicles to drive to the Dan Marino Stadium for the game.

"Mom, you should see all the comments of people who stood in agreement with us. You know prayers are more effective with others interceding," Gya explained.

"Just don't let this ministry turn into an idol. I feel like you've become obsessed with social media. Please be careful. You know how fickle the public is. They love you one minute and hate you the next. Remember the *I Said Yes* fiasco? I don't want to see you hurt again, Gya."

Gya smiled and kissed her mom's cheek. "I'll be fine, Mom. Trust me. I got this."

The Waves had a blowout win against the Jacksonville Jaguars. After the game, once Bryant had finished his post-game interviews, the family went to have a celebratory dinner at Il Gabbiano, an upscale restaurant that specialized in Italian cuisine.

Once they were seated, Gya went live once again. "Give it up for my baby, y'all." Gya smiled into the camera before panning it to Bryant who had a stellar first game with two touchdowns.

"Gya, can you please put that phone away?" her mother asked in a voice tight with annoyance.

"Great game, Bryant. May I please have your autograph?" A young white male fan approached their table with a napkin and pen.

"I'm sorry, but my husband doesn't sign autographs during meals," Gya told the fan.

"No problem, my man," Bryant said, ignoring Gya and signing the fan's napkin. He also posed for a photo with him.

The fan thanked him before returning to his table.

Gya caught the entire exchange on livestream, but she turned the camera to face her. "My husband was gracious enough to oblige the gentleman, but in the future if you see Bryant and me dining at a restaurant, I kindly ask that you not interrupt our meal seeking autographs and photos. It's rather intrusive and rude."

"No more intrusive than you having that damn camera in everyone's faces while we're at the table," Bryant said, glaring at Gya.

Taken aback at his profane language and his tone, Gya abruptly ended the livestream, and a tense silence fell over the table.

"Bryant...I don't appreciate you talking to me like that."

"And I don't appreciate you being rude to a fan. You made me look like a real simp, trying to dictate when I should sign autographs. Don't ever do that again."

Tears of shame and humiliation stung Gya's eyes. Excusing herself, she made a hasty retreat to the ladies' room. Once inside, the tears of hurt poured forth. The door to the ladies' room opened as her mother followed her in.

"Gya, I warned you that you were going overboard with the livestreams," Pam said, pulling her in for a comforting hug.

"Is Dad at the table tearing into Bryant for how he talked to me?"

"No, ma'am. Your father and I are staying out of this. As long as Bryant doesn't put his hands on you, we are staying out of any arguments or disagreements between the two of you. But I will say I agree with Bryant to a certain extent. You were out of line to try and check his fan. It was considerably rude and off-putting. Now I'm all for establishing boundaries, but there's a correct way to go about it. What I just witnessed at the dinner table wasn't it."

Gya took a few more moments to gather her bearings before returning to the table. She avoided Bryant's eyes, and the two proceeded to ignore each other for the remainder of the dinner, which made for a rather awkward atmosphere. At one point, a group of exotic-looking females approached the table and spoke to Bryant but the look of death Gya shot at them was their cue to keep the niceties short and not linger.

After dinner, they drove both families to the airport to catch their return flights home to Houston.

"I'm praying you and Bryant can settle this. Please don't go to bed angry with each other," Pam said before giving Gya a hug and a kiss goodbye. Gya hugged and kissed her father, along with Bryant's parents and sister. Once all were inside of the airport, she and Bryant pulled away, and they drove a few miles in silence.

"So do you want to hash this out?" Bryant finally said.

"Yes. I'm waiting on your apology for humiliating me."

"Gya, I'm the one who felt disrespected. How are you the victim here?"

"Speaking of disrespect, you should've checked those thirsty females for flirting with you in my face. I don't appreciate the way they spoke to you but ignored me."

"Gya, *I'm* the celebrity, not you. Baby, I thought you could handle what this lifestyle entailed, but you're not doing a very good job. Honestly, I think that's why you even started this Well Worth the Wait nonsense. It's your way of ensuring you're never in my shadow."

"*Nonsense*? Your *shadow*? Boy, if you don't get over yourself. You know good and well I started this ministry in college years ago so why is it a problem now?"

"I didn't realize it would start consuming so much of your time."

"Because that's less time I have to focus on you and kissing your behind like all of your adoring fans, right?"

Bryant exhaled long and loud, turning up the volume on the Drake song playing via a Sirius XM satellite station. Gya noticed Bryant had started listening to rap a lot more since joining the NFL. They rode the remainder of the way home in silence except for the blaring music.

Gya had a massive headache, which she figured was a combination of their argument and the trash music she was forced to listen to for the duration of the ride home. She went upstairs to take a nice hot bath while Bryant settled into the den to watch game day highlights on *SportsCenter.*

The warmth of the water nearly caused Gya to doze off right in the tub, but she was instantly alert once Bryant entered the bathroom with a bottle of wine and a tray of chocolate-covered strawberries Gya kept on hand in their fridge. Two empty wine flutes were also on the tray.

"A peace offering?" Bryant said, giving her his sexy, irresistible grin as he knelt beside the tub. He captured her lips in a kiss. "I'm willing to be the bigger person here. I'm sorry I hurt you, baby."

"I'm sorry you felt I disrespected or emasculated you. That was never my intent," Gya acquiesced.

Bryant kissed her once again before disrobing and joining her in the tub. They capped off the eventful evening with round after round of makeup sex.

***

Bryant Green Puts Wife in Check Live on Camera!
This was the headline of a story posted on The Shade Room, which recapped yesterday's dinner fiasco, including footage from the livestream of Bryant going off on Gya. Tatum had texted Gya the link before phoning to ask if all was well, which Gya assured her it was. Their argument was a hiccup all marriages faced, and Gya decided to make a point of ignoring the gossip blogs this time around.

Gya and Bryant were having breakfast before he reported to the team facility for a workout and to watch some game film. He was tuned in to *SportsCenter* once again when the sports commentator reported breaking news out of Miami.

"Miami Waves wide receiver Tyrik Fisher has been arrested this morning after surveillance video captured him assaulting his girlfriend in the parking lot of a hotel along the Las Vegas strip. The assault occurred last weekend..."

Both Bryant and Gya looked at each other in astonishment as the commentator droned on. They'd seen both Tyrik and his girlfriend, Giselle, at yesterday's game, and they were carrying on like normal. Tyrik also played a great game.

"If this happened last weekend, why is he just now being arrested?" Gya questioned after the breaking news report concluded.

"I'll bet you an employee of the hotel leaked the footage in exchange for some cash," Bryant surmised.

"Wow. This is not good. I must say, I have now lost all respect for Tyrik. I never thought he was a woman beater."

"Let's not rush to judgment, Gya. Why don't we wait for more details to emerge?"

"Bryant, there's video, and if the police arrested him, then they have sufficient evidence. The Waves need to kick him off the team. Better yet, I hope he's banned from the NFL for good. Like I said, I have no respect for guys who beat up on women."

Bryant decided to head to the team facility so he could get more information on what was going on with his teammate. Pretty soon, social media and news outlets were buzzing as the surveillance video was released. Gya was sick to her stomach as she witnessed Tyrik push Giselle to the ground and then proceed to kick her.

"Yeah, buddy, you're finished," Gya said under her breath. She decided to go live, as she'd planned to issue an apology to her followers for the disagreement they'd witnessed between her and Bryant. But she also wanted to hold a discussion about Tyrik's arrest and gather thoughts about the issue of domestic violence.

The livestream lasted two hours. Gya wasn't shy in sharing her opinion about Tyrik being banished from the league. She also discussed a possible boycott of NFL games if the league tried to give Tyrik a slap on the wrist, and many followers agreed that black women needed to be protected and not have instances of violence against them be treated lightly and brushed under the rug.

Once Gya ended the livestream, Victor Moore's wife, Christal, phoned her.

"Gya, I'm gonna be honest: I just talked to Victor, and team personnel has caught wind of your livestream. They are not happy that you went forward with discussing this. I know you're new to this lifestyle, but certain team matters aren't to be shared so openly with the public."

"Tyrik is a monster, Christal. Didn't you see how he kicked Giselle like she was some mangy dog? I thought you'd have her back."

"I do have her back, but I'm not for publicly bashing Waves players."

"Well, I guess we'll just have to agree to disagree," Gya said.

When Bryant arrived home later that evening, he echoed Christal's sentiments. "Once again, you've embarrassed me, Gya. Team personnel think I can't handle my wife. No more live videos, Gya. I mean it," Bryant said, his voice adamant and firm.

"Excuse me?"

"You heard what I said. This whole ministry thing of yours has been nothing but trouble. Can't you see that? Why do you always have to be so opinionated? I'm tired of you holding me by the balls. I defended you during the *I Said Yes* interview controversy, but even then, you were speaking over me and answering questions before I could get a word in. No more of this, Gya. It stops today."

"Look, Bryant, I'm real tired of this whole macho man routine of yours. So, you want to rule over me, is that it? Let's get this clear: I am not stopping my livestreams. It's ministry. Don't you get that?"

"Isn't submission one of your godly principles?" Bryant shot back. "It's in the book of Ephesians, right—wives honoring their husbands?"

Gya had no comeback.

"Yeah, don't get all tongue-tied now. It's funny how all the godliness 101 flies out the window once it's time for you to walk the talk."

"Bryant, I didn't intend to bash Tyrik with that livestream. It was just a mere discussion about what happened. And yes, some of my followers went in on him for his actions, and I can understand their frustration. Because you've come to consider Tyrik as a friend, you may feel a bit biased—"

"There you go again. You don't think for me, Gya. You still don't understand that, do you?"

"Bryant, calm down."

"Nah, I'm chill. I've got nothing else to say."

Bryant stomped upstairs to their guest bedroom. He never returned to their room that night. Gya lay alone in their bed and eventually cried herself to sleep.

Chapter Eleven

"Lord," Tatum began with her palms together and her eyes closed as she knelt on the side of her plush king-sized bed. "I know you don't approve of King and me living in sin. God, if you want us to stop fornicating, please move on King's heart and get him to propose to me."

"Tatum!"

Tatum's eyes shot open as she heard King yell out for her as he walked into the apartment. She immediately stood to her feet.

Dang, God, you're gonna answer my prayer that quick?

Tatum rushed out of their bedroom and found King in the kitchen holding an ice pack to his right eye.

"Baby, what happened?" Tatum asked when she saw the black bruising around his eye, the flesh surrounding the area swelling up.

"Wesley Johnson. He and I had it out at practice. Dude has been digging at me since I was drafted. I'm tired of it."

"King, you got into a fight with your teammate?"

"I busted his nose," King boasted.

Antoine's wife, Kelsea, had revealed to Tatum that there had been a lot of tension between King and some of the veteran Flash players. Many of them found King cocky and arrogant. Tatum felt they were threatened and jealous, and Kelsea agreed. Tatum was glad that Kelsea and Ariana's husbands were willing to befriend King and take him under their wings for mentoring. Wesley Johnson didn't have the best reputation with the Flash organization—or with the NBA period. He was often on the trading block because of his poor attitude. Tatum reasoned Wesley didn't take too much of a liking to King because they shared a lot of the same mannerisms, both very egotistical.

Tatum went over to kiss and soothe him. "Make sure you keep the ice on it."

She was livid that Wesley was acting like a big bully and picking fights with King, who was much younger.

King ended up nodding off on the couch for an afternoon nap. Tatum discovered that *SportsCenter* had already picked up news about the scuffle between Wesley and King. She reflected on her past argument regarding birth control with her mom, along with her expectations that King take care of her. But all had been rectified when Vanessa called to make amends. Her mother apologized for being overbearing, and Tatum accepted, glad they could put it all behind them.

Once King awakened, Tatum ordered in dinner, continuing her pampering of him by preparing his plate once it arrived.

"I'm my own man from now on. I ain't gonna be hanging too hard with the rest of the team while here in NYC or when we're out on the road," King said, digging into a piece of seared salmon.

"Baby, no man is an island. It would be good for you to try and get along with your teammates," Tatum advised, sipping a glass of wine.

"Tatum, this isn't elementary school. The NBA is not a sandbox. I don't owe those dudes anything. I'm just there to ball and that's it. I ain't trying to make no friends. Self-preservation is the first law of nature. My father has always instilled that slogan within me. I'm cool with being a beast on the court, making my millions and going about my business."

I hope that business includes placing a ring on my finger soon, Tatum thought as her earlier prayer came to mind again.

"Well, the Flash and the Waves have been keeping the sports world busy. Between your scuffle with Wesley and Tyrik Fisher's arrest, they have plenty of headlines," Tatum said.

"Man, Tyrik is an idiot. He should know by now there are cameras everywhere. You rough up your girl behind closed doors, not out in public."

Tatum nearly choked on her wine. "King, are you serious right now? You don't rough up your girlfriend or wife, *period*."

"Tay, chill out. I'm not justifying him hitting her."

"It sure sounds like it."

"Have I ever put my hands on you?"

"No, and you'd better not ever start. I'm telling you, King: You have one time to hit me, and I'm gone."

King smirked. "You ain't going nowhere, Tatum."

"Boy, try me," Tatum said, feeling herself growing heated.

"Okay, okay, I'm just messing with you, girl. Calm down," King said, reaching over for her hand.

Tatum jerked away and began clearing the table.

"So now you got an attitude?"

"It's best I get out of your way before you make me curse you out."

"Don't be like that," King said, pinching her behind as she walked by with their empty plates in hand.

"I'm not playing with you, King," Tatum said.

King continued to chuckle and then went into the living room to start playing on his PS5 game system.

As Tatum loaded the dishwasher, she thought about King's words about Tyrik and him stating she would never leave him. She felt as if he took her for granted. But she was serious about not putting up with any domestic abuse. She'd be on the first thing smoking back home to Houston if he ever assaulted her.

After cleaning the kitchen, Tatum went to shower, thinking about how Gya was again being blasted on social media for speaking out against Tyrik. Tatum was proud of her cousin and shared her convictions. She was also glad that Gya wasn't letting the nasty comments by armchair critics get under her skin this time around.

King soon made his way into the bedroom and cuddled up underneath Tatum. She caved and gave in to his hot and feverish kisses, and they succumbed to making love. When it was over, Tatum still underwent feelings of guilt, yet she felt helpless to stop fulfilling the desires of her flesh.

***

Gya and Bryant were called into team headquarters to stand before the head coach, the team owner, and other team personnel. Gya was told in no uncertain terms to stop discussing Waves team matters to the public. With tightened lips, she agreed and apologized, leaving the offices feeling like a chastened child. She was upset with herself for caving, but she kept Bryant's interests in mind. But the Waves organization had a lot of nerve thinking they could put a muzzle on her.

Bryant still hadn't said more than two words to her since their argument the night before. He didn't bother to kiss or tell her goodbye as they exited the offices. Instead, he headed toward the weight room, and Gya ventured out to her Porsche and drove home, crying softly the entire drive while listening to the powerful yet soothing voice of Tamela Mann as she belted out the lyrics of the song "Help Me." Once back at their home, Gya went into prayer for resolution to this disagreement with Bryant.

Christal came over later that afternoon.

"You know, the other WAGs are saying you're using Tyrik and Giselle as scapegoats to deflect attention away from your argument with Bryant at the restaurant last Sunday." WAGs was the popular acronym used to refer to the wives and girlfriends of pro athletes.

"They can think whatever they want. That's far from the truth. After all, I didn't tell Tyrik to beat up his girlfriend. I see people on social media saying things along the same lines, such as I'm using this situation to bring in more followers. I don't have to do all that. When you're led by God, you don't have to resort to tricks and gimmicks."

Gya decided she'd had enough of the Waves WAGs and resolved to only associate with Christal moving forward. She didn't need their negativity within her life. She shared her thoughts with Christal.

"Can I be honest? The girls aren't really feeling you either. Since meeting you that evening on the yacht, they got snooty vibes from you. Many of them feel as if you think you're better than everyone else, but I didn't let that sway me from hanging out with you."

"Glad you can think for yourself," Gya said, her feelings not at all hurt by the WAGs' snub and dismissal of her. She decided she'd just sit with Christal during home games going forward.

When Bryant returned from practice later that evening, Gya had a delicious home-cooked meal prepared that consisted of southern favorites Bryant's mother used to make for him such as fried chicken, green beans, and baked mac and cheese. By the way his eyes lit up when he entered the kitchen, Gya could tell he approved.

She went to him and enveloped him in a hug, which he returned.

"There's been so much tension between us since the season started. The devil is hard at work within our lives, baby, but he's got the wrong ones. No way in hell will I allow him to drive a wedge into this marriage."

Bryant smiled and kissed her on the forehead.

"A forehead kiss? Seriously?" Gya teased.

"Oh, I don't think you're ready for anything deeper."

"I'll show you how ready I am after dinner. Just make sure you make your way back into our bedroom tonight."

They spent dinner chattering, and Gya felt herself relax, glad for the sense of normalcy that returned between them. And she kept her word, showing Bryant well into the night just how sorry she was.

Chapter Twelve

The NBA season began in October, and King's family, along with Tatum's mother, Vanessa, flew in to cheer King on for his first pro game. Even his brother, Korey, was in attendance.

Kelsea had schooled Tatum on what Flash personnel expected of the wives. Like LA, New York City was an entertainment magnet, and Kelsea told Tatum to bring her A-game as far as her appearance and attire. Cameras may do a sweep of the stands and capture her on television, introducing her as King's girlfriend. She could also find herself on the jumbotron. Vanessa decided to put just as much effort into her appearance, getting Tatum to take her on an impromptu shopping spree earlier that evening on Fifth Avenue. She cited she didn't want to be an embarrassment to her daughter and future son-in-law, so she wanted to be dressed to the nines as well.

During halftime, Vanessa and Tatum found themselves seated alone once King's family went to take a restroom break and visit the various concession areas of the Pat Riley arena. Tatum had introduced her mother to Kelsea and Ariana earlier, and her mother had taken a liking to both.

"You know, I went to a lot of preseason games, and I was surprised to see that many athletes have black women on their arms. The league is not oversaturated with interracial relationships as I initially thought. It just seems like those are the relationships the mainstream media chooses to highlight," Tatum said.

"And you know exactly why that is. White and light is right in their book. You're just as beautiful as those other exotic-looking women, and don't you ever forget that. Just remember to always keep your appearance on point, and don't let the media catch you half stepping. Have you talked to Gya lately?" Vanessa asked.

"Yeah. She said the other wives and girlfriends have pretty much frozen her out. She mostly keeps to herself at games now."

Vanessa shook her head. "I can't say I'm surprised. I've watched a few of her videos. Like I said once before, Gya has an air about her that screams, *I'm better than you.* She comes by it honestly, coming from such a pompous family."

Tatum changed the subject before Vanessa started ranting about her father, Charles.

"King has gotten off to a slow start since the preseason. I know he's still trying to adjust to the league. The media has already started going in on him, saying he might not live up to his contract and will be a bust. Not to mention he and Wesley Johnson are still not on good terms. They barely say two words to each other."

"That Wesley fella is just jealous because he knows King is a good player, once he finds his rhythm. I can't wait for King to show them what's he really made of. Trust me, he's not an NCAA champion for nothing. He'll get it together. Just continue to be his biggest cheerleader," Vanessa encouraged.

"What I'm seeing and hearing in the media isn't all bad though. *People* magazine did a feature on him, discussing his boyishly handsome looks and calling him the newest heartthrob. They even wrote that he could be voted next year's Sexiest Man Alive. Mom, I'm gonna be honest: I'm a bit nervous about all these thirsty females out here. You should've seen them all trying to gain access to the team parking area after the preseason games. I love King, but I'm not gonna stand around and be cheated on constantly. I won't be made a fool of."

Vanessa turned to look her daughter in the eye. "King comes home to you, and that's all that matters, Tatum. Your cousin Natasha is being cheated on by a dude who lives with her and doesn't even work. Now *that's* foolish. You and I both know what type of lifestyles these athletes lead when they're out on the road. I'm gonna give it to you straight: You're with a multi-millionaire so there's nothing wrong with turning a blind eye to a few indiscretions."

"So, I should be okay with him cheating?"

"It's like I told you once before: Don't sweat the small stuff. And another thing, Kelsea and Ariana are cool enough, but try to keep a low profile and not hang around too many other of the wives or girlfriends. That's an invitation to drama because they'll be smiling in your face while discussing King's dalliances behind your back. And some of those heffas are even bold enough to try and creep with him, too, especially if the baller they're with ends up kicking them to the curb. Yes, always keep both eyes open, Tatum. Do not trust any of these females and remember to keep an air of mystery about yourself. It'll make the media more curious about you. Gya is an open book, airing all of her and

Bryant's business out in the streets with those silly little vlogs. I'm telling you, it's gonna end up backfiring on her," Vanessa advised.

King's family returning to take their seats marked the end of the conversation, and Tatum spent the second half silently mulling over everything she and her mother discussed. The Flash ended up winning the season opener with King averaging fifteen points. He seemed to be a bit embarrassed when he met up with them after the game.

"You guys came all the way to New York only to see me bring in high school numbers," King said.

His mother gave him a hug of reassurance. "I'm still so proud of you."

Even Korey gave his big brother a fist bump while Jacoby patted his eldest son on the back. "You're gonna end up killing it out there, son, and be a household name one day soon, I guarantee it. Now let's go get some post-game grub."

Everyone laughed, and King told Tatum to order food in, as he really wasn't in the mood to be mobbed at a restaurant, and Tatum agreed. A nice dinner at home surrounded by family was the makings of a perfect end to her day.

***

"No weapon formed against me or my marriage will prosper. Though people slay me with their tongues, I'll still serve the Lord."

Gya smiled at the standing ovation and thunderous applause that followed her proclamation. She sat in her home office and watched a re-play of the women's empowerment conference that was held at ONE Church Los Angeles a few weeks ago. Gya's segment had set the place on fire with praise and worship. Each time she reflected on the conference, she got chills at the move of God that went forth. She was still in awe and amazed at how God used her during that conference.

All the turmoil that was present within her life at the time had since passed. Tyrik was released from the Waves following the domestic dispute and was a free agent, but given the controversy, no NFL team wanted to risk signing him. Tyrik was convinced that his release from the Waves came in part of the team and league fearing a boycott and protests on behalf of women's rights associations. Tyrik believed it was Gya who fueled the waging war against him

60

and his character. Word had it that he vowed that both Bryant and Gya were his enemies for life, as he'd never forgive her for the role she played in ruining his NFL career and reputation.

His girlfriend Giselle was just as upset, citing that Gya should've minded her own business. But Giselle was roasted in the press and online for staying with Tyrik and not being willing to pursue charges against him for his assault. Giselle made it clear that she was standing by her man and didn't want him to serve any jail time.

Gya could only shake her head, as she felt Tyrik had a lot of nerve in trying to shift blame onto her for his poor choices, but she continued to keep them both uplifted in prayer.

Gya was glad all the drama was behind them now, and she felt herself bubble with excitement at hearing Bryant's car pull into the driveway. She grabbed her phone and went live on Instagram as she went to greet him.

Upon entering the house and seeing Gya holding the phone in his face, Bryant groaned and rolled his eyes. "Gya, are you serious right now?"

"C'mon and follow me into the kitchen, silly. I have a surprise for you," Gya said, giggling.

Bryant followed his wife as directed, and once inside of their spacious kitchen, he spotted two onesies on top of their kitchen island. The word *boy* was written on the front of one of the onesies while *girl* was written on the other. Bryant glanced at Gya in confusion, and then his eyes lit up when he realized the message she was trying to convey.

"Babe, are you pregnant?"

"Yes indeed, baby. We're gonna be parents."

Bryant let out a shout and lifted Gya off her feet, causing her to fumble the phone.

"Bryant, babe, did you forget we're live?" Gya said, unable to control her laughter at his excitement.

"I don't care. I'm gonna be a daddy."

He and Gya shared a kiss, and Gya glanced at her phone to see a plethora of congratulatory comments and emojis. She turned the camera to face her and thanked everyone for their well wishes.

"My due date is next summer, and I thank God that I'm delivering during the NFL off season so Bryant can be present to witness the birth of our first child with no game day distractions. Now if you'll excuse me, I'm logging off now to continue to celebrate this blessed news with my husband. Thank you all again for your prayers, love, and outpouring of support." Gya signed off.

Bryant smiled and grabbed her by the hand, leading her upstairs to their bedroom. Gya assumed that he'd try to make love, but Bryant merely spooned with her on the bed, his hand resting lovingly against her belly, which would soon fill out even more with their child, before drifting into an afternoon nap.

Chapter Thirteen

Gya handed her keys to the valet and strode inside Prime 112. Upon entering the restaurant, she informed the hostess that her party was expecting her. The hostess nodded and led Gya to a table where two women named Brittany and Greer were seated. Brittany was the wife of Waves defensive end Dion Fletcher, and Greer was engaged to the fullback, Gary Preston.

Gya was beyond surprised when Brittany reached out to her, wanting to extend an olive branch on behalf of the other Waves WAGs. She acknowledged they'd gotten off on the wrong foot at the team's yacht party this past summer and wanted Gya to have lunch with her and Greer so they could get to know her better. Gya was humbled and readily agreed.

She now flashed a genuine smile of greeting at the two beautiful ladies as she sat down, requesting that the waiter bring her a glass of strawberry lemonade.

"Thank you so much for coming, Gya," Brittany said by way of greeting.

"It's my pleasure," Gya responded, taking in Brittany's thick and lustrous natural curls. "Your hair is beautiful. Every time I see you, it's always so coily and full of bounce." Gya laughed.

"Oh, thank you, girl," Brittany said, playfully twirling a strand of her hair. "Miss Jessie's products keep these curls popping."

"And how are you, Greer?" Gya greeted, smiling in turn at the statuesque blonde who looked as if she could model for a Colgate ad with her shimmering blond hair and translucent emerald-green eyes.

"I'm well, Gya. Thanks for asking," Greer said, handing Gya one of the menus to peruse.

"I'm gonna be honest: I don't fancy steakhouses. I'm trying to lay off beef, but this grilled salmon and lobster tail meal sounds delicious."

Gya looked up to see Brittany and Greer exchange glances.

"My apologies, ladies. I'm not trying to come off pretentious."

"No, it's not that. Look, I'm gonna be transparent. There's another reason we asked you to lunch today," Brittany said.

Gya frowned at the tone of unease she detected in Brittany's voice. "What's going on?"

Brittany took a deep breath. "There are some murmurings within the Waves organization of a paternity suit being filed against Bryant."

Gya gaped at Brittany for a couple of seconds and then laughed. "Are you serious right now? Brittany, I can assure you the only child Bryant is expecting is the one growing in my belly. Who told you this foolishness?"

"Gya, paternity suits are commonplace within the league. I know you have this whole Polly Purity thing going with your little ministry and all, but please don't be jaded and naïve," Brittany said.

"Look, for a paternity suit to even be a possibility that means Bryant has cheated on me, and I can assure you that hasn't happened. We're newlyweds, for goodness' sakes. I mean, when would he even have had the time to step out on me? You're gonna have to come better, and I don't appreciate you wasting my time, bringing me here under the guise of friendship only to sit and gossip about a silly and unsubstantiated rumor."

"Bri, let me take over from here. Gya, us WAGs try to have a united front with one another and stick together when we learn of infidelity. We brought you here with good intentions because we wanted to break the news to you before it leaked to the media. I can see Bryant hasn't shared any of this with you," Greer spoke up.

"Because it's not true. Why would he come to me with such nonsense?"

"Look, I can see you're getting upset, but please don't turn a blind eye to this. As much as we realize how much it will hurt you, we want you to know the *entire* truth. The female behind the paternity suit is Mercedes," Brittany said.

Gya's eyes widened in incredulity. "Christal's little cousin Mercedes? Now I know this is a joke. Christal would've mentioned this to me."

Brittany raised an eyebrow. "Would she? You don't think she'd cover for her family?"

Gya stood and angrily grabbed her purse. "I've lost my appetite. This was a mistake, and I should've known better than to trust you. I really thought you two wanted to make amends, but you brought me here with treacherous intentions."

"Oh, grow up, Gya. The only one you can't trust is your husband," Brittany said.

"Go to hell, Brittany, and stay away from me. Both of you."

"Wow, such godly language," Greer said, with a derisive chuckle.

It took everything within Gya to refrain from grabbing her glass of strawberry lemonade and tossing the drink in both of their faces. Instead, she spun on her heels and stormed out of the restaurant.

Outside, she practically barked at the valet to bring her car around as quickly as possible. Once inside of her Porsche Panamera, she activated her Bluetooth system with trembling fingers to call Bryant. It went to voicemail. Needing to talk to someone, Gya dialed up Tatum. As soon as her cousin answered, Gya's voice trembled with tears and anger as she filled Tatum in on what transpired.

"So, do you think they're lying? Gya, don't be upset with me, but I don't believe they'd invite you to lunch just to taunt you with lies. The Flash WAGs are the same way. We all try to look out for each other. These rumors didn't just emerge from out of nowhere, and I don't put anything past this Christal either. She is more than likely aware too. My mom said you have to be careful around certain women because they're undercover snakes. You need to talk to Bryant as soon as possible to get to the bottom of this. Confront Christal too. You deserve answers from her as well," Tatum advised.

Tatum talked to Gya for the duration of the drive back to her home, and Christal beeped in on the other line just as Gya pulled into her driveway.

"Speak of the devil. This is Christal calling me now. I bet you Brittany and Greer filled her in on everything. They are probably all in this together now that I think about it. Let me call you back, cousin."

"Yes. Be sure you do because I want to hear what that skank has to say for herself," Tatum said.

Christal was full of apologies once Gya answered.

"You have to understand the awkward situation I was in, Gya. Family is family, and even though what Mercedes did was wrong, I still want to always have her back."

"So, are you telling me she actually slept with Bryant? This is crazy. How and when did this happen?" Gya asked, her eyes filling with tears of betrayal.

"It happened this summer during training camp. Look, I'll leave it to Bryant to fill you in on everything."

"Is she really pregnant?"

"I mean, that's what she's saying."

"If it happened this summer, then that means she's about three months along. Why is she just now saying something?"

"She told me about it right after it happened."

"And you've been smiling in my face since then?"

"So has Bryant. Don't try to come for *me*, Gya. You need to be checking him," Christal said, her words mirroring Brittany's.

Gya hung up in Christal's face and began to beat the steering wheel, releasing a slow, painful wail of hurt, confusion, and anger. Burning tears streamed down her face as she rested her head against the steering wheel and sobbed her heart out. How could Bryant do something like this?

Her phone rang, and she saw it was Tatum.

"Gya, TMZ has already posted the story about the paternity suit. The headline claims he has two babies on the way," Tatum informed her. "Dammit, I see The Shade Room and WAGs Unfiltered have posted about it too. I bet you those two wenches leaked this story as soon as you left the restaurant."

Gya's body went numb. She felt so alone and no longer knew who she could trust.

"Tay, I gotta go. I–I need to wrap my head around all this."

"Do you need me to fly into Miami? I can be there in a few hours."

"I appreciate the offer, cousin, but—I just need some time. I–I just don't know."

"Okay, well, I'll give you some space, but please call me, Gya. I'm always here, and I love you so much. You're gonna get through this, I promise."

Gya told her she loved her, too, and hung up, walking into the house on autopilot. She was tempted to call Bryant again, but she decided it would be best to be able to look into his eyes when he finally explained this huge mess. Gya told Alexa to play Smokie Norful's "I Need You Now" and then she fell to her knees in her den in prayer, crying out to God for answers and to bring some kind of solace because she was hurt beyond comprehension.

Gya's mom called, but Gya let it go to voicemail because her mom would demand answers—the same answers Gya was seeking. She didn't want to talk to anyone now except for Bryant.

He finally came trudging through the door an hour or so later, holding a bag that Gya knew contained empanadas and a slice of key lime pie, two of her favorite desserts since moving to Miami. He often came home surprising her with the treats. Gya's heart sank when he could barely meet her eyes, and she couldn't believe he thought desserts could serve as peace offering in this instance. When he extended the bag, Gya yanked it from his grasp, ripping it open and throwing the desserts at him. Bryant's eyes widened at her display of rage, then he swallowed and released a long exhale, running his hands over his face.

"Gya...baby...I–I'm so sorry."

"Sorry for what, Bryant? A part of me was holding out hope that this wasn't true. Are you about to stand here and confess to me that not only did you cheat on me but with Mercedes of all people? You actually cheated on me a month within our marriage? Is that what you're standing here telling me?"

Bryant flinched at the escalation of her voice.

"Baby, please, calm down. I don't want you upsetting the baby."

"*Which* baby, Bryant?" Gya taunted.

Bryant could only drop his head. "Look, for what it's worth, I don't believe she's pregnant, and I don't believe it's mine."

"It shouldn't even be a possibility. You know what, just get the hell out of my face. All I'm hearing is your sorry apologies and denials. The BS excuses are not far behind, and I'm not here for it. Stay the hell away from me, Bryant. As a matter of fact, I'm not even staying here tonight. I need to be as far away from you as possible."

"Wait, Gya. At least let me explain to you what happened. It was just some craziness during training camp. Some of the other players were teasing me about my good-boy image. When I returned to my room that night, Mercedes was sitting on my bed waiting for me. It was all arranged by Victor. She'd told him she had a huge crush on me since meeting me at your party. Gya, I promised I tried to get her to leave, but she first threatened to spread a rumor that I was secretly gay if I didn't sleep with her. She said people would believe it and assume that's how you and I were able to go so long without having sex. Then she said she'd accuse me of sexually assaulting her. Baby, I was scared. I didn't need my reputation to take a hit, and I didn't want to be marred in any controversy so soon after being drafted."

"And yet here we are. You compromised our marriage just because you didn't want your manhood questioned?"

"Gya, what if I was accused of rape? You know how serious those kinds of allegations are? I would've been roasted in the court of public opinion. No one would've believed she was lying. You see what those women groups did to Tyrik's career, prodded in part by you, I might add."

"Don't you dare try to turn this around on me, Bryant. This is about you and your transgression against our marriage. You should've just left the room and taken your chances, but no, you didn't. It's because a part of you wanted to sleep with her, didn't you? Go ahead admit it, Bryant. You were turned on by her, weren't you?"

Bryant dropped his head again, and Gya felt like someone had a grip on her heart and was wrenching it. It felt like a painful dagger.

"You can't even deny it, huh, Bryant? Wow, I guess Brittany and Greer were right. I *am* naïve. I thought you only had eyes for me."

"I do, Gya. You're still my one and only. Nothing will change that."

"Oh, I beg to differ. This child that Mercedes is carrying serves as a permanent reminder of your betrayal. Look, let me go pack a bag and get out of here."

"No, Gya, you don't have to leave. I don't want you and our child somewhere out on the streets of Miami. I'll leave."

"Are you going to go lay up with Mercedes again? Have you been creeping around with her, Bryant?"

"No. I promise it was that one time."

"That's all it took to get her pregnant. I can't believe you didn't use a condom. You could've given me an STD."

"I didn't have any protection on hand because it wasn't planned. Can't you see that?"

"All I can see is you having sex with her, and it makes me sick to my stomach. I hate you so much right now, Bryant. I never thought I'd utter those words to you, and especially not four months within our marriage." With a sob, Gya ran upstairs to their bedroom, slamming the door behind her and falling upon the bed in another fit of tears.

***

She awakened hours later with swollen, puffy eyes and a pounding headache. Gya sat up and listened. The house was eerily silent, which meant that Bryant had left. She was both relieved and heart broken. She couldn't deal with him right now, yet she was devastated that the future of their marriage now hung in the balance. A marriage that was so fresh and new. What did this mean for the future of the child growing in her womb?

Grabbing her cell phone, Gya saw that she had over thirty missed calls. She recognized her mother and Tatum, but there were some from numbers she didn't recognize, which left her to ponder if reps from certain news outlets and gossip blogs had gained access to her cell phone number. She had just as many voicemails, which she was in no mood to listen to and sort through. Gya decided to finally call her mother back.

"Gya, thank goodness. I was just packing my bags and about to book a flight to Miami. Your father has been trying to talk me out of flying in, telling me you are a married woman now and to let you and Bryant handle your issues as husband and wife, but I was worried sick when I couldn't reach you."

"I apologize, Mom. I just needed some time and space to get my head together," Gya said, all the while thinking how her afternoon nap did nothing to calm her nerves.

"Baby, say the word, and I'll be down there."

"No, Mom. Dad is right. Bryant and I need to handle this on our own."

"Well, just know both of you are in our prayers. And I shouldn't have to tell you this, but please don't hesitate to pick up the phone and call me for anything. If you need to scream, cry, yell, vent, call me, baby. Is there anything I can do?"

"You've said it already, Mom. Just pray."

"Will do. I love you, sweetheart, and in spite of his mistake, I still love Bryant too. I'm praying you guys make it through this."

Telling her mom she loved her as well, Gya hung up, not sure if she shared her mother's hopes about pulling through this situation with Bryant.

Chapter Fourteen

Gya ended up crying herself to sleep once again, and when she awakened the next morning, the events of the previous day came flooding back to her remembrance in a depressing wave. She could hear the sound of *SportsCenter* playing from the television downstairs, so Bryant had made his way back home but he didn't sleep in their room. Gya never imagined they'd again be sleeping in separate bedrooms so soon into their marriage. None of what was occurring was within her dreams for their marriage. She was in a living nightmare.

Gya showered and then made her way downstairs. She wanted to avoid Bryant, not even wanting to look him in his lying and deceitful eyes, but he cornered her in the kitchen. He went to move toward her, extending his arms, but Gya's death stare stopped him in his tracks.

"I can't apologize enough, baby."

"You're right. You can't," Gya spat.

"Tell me what I have to do to make this right."

"You can't, Bryant," she repeated. "You have a whole baby on the way with another woman. You have two women knocked up at the same time. I'm so disgusted by you. I haven't been online, but I can only imagine how much of a laughingstock I am right now. How am I supposed to face my followers? I've spoken so glowingly of you and our marriage and now this?"

"So that's what you're concerned about? Your image?"

"Yes, and you should be too. Both of us look foolish, Bryant."

"I don't care about all that stupid stuff, Gya. No one told you to go and make our marriage a walking billboard for a godly relationship."

"And you just don't know how much I regret it. You know, my grandmother used to always say a woman should never brag too much about her man or her children because they will make a straight fool out of you. I learned the hard way her words are true. Just get out of my face, Bryant. I'm going to be talking to a lawyer today about an annulment."

Bryant's eyes widened. "Wow, so just like that you bail at the first sign of trouble? There's no way we can work this out?"

"Don't you go trying to lay a guilt trip on me. You bailed on this marriage as soon as you decided to lay down with Mercedes." With one last glare, Gya left the kitchen, stomping up the stairs and slamming their bedroom door.

***

"...so in closing, I'm going to be honest and state that I don't know what the future of my marriage entails. But I know God calls us to forgive, so as hard as it may be, I must find it within my heart to forgive my husband."

Tatum watched as Gya wiped tears from her eyes during her livestream video, which was broadcast on Instagram, Facebook and YouTube.

"Since starting Well Worth the Wait, I promised to always be real and authentic with my followers, which is why I had to give a statement concerning these allegations of Bryant impregnating another woman. I'm not one to run and hide in shame. Also, I've seen comments that I've tried to paint the picture that my marriage was perfect, which was never my intent. I just ask that you keep me in your prayers. And you know what, I pray now for the woman my husband engaged in the act of adultery with, as well as the alleged child growing within her belly. I extend my forgiveness and prayers to her. I will not publicly bash her, and I ask my followers to refrain from doing the same. Well Worth the Wait is about sisterhood and empowerment, not trashing and bashing. Thank you all for tuning in. God bless."

Tatum sighed, feeling that Gya had lost her mind in praying for this Mercedes chick. In her eyes, there wasn't that much love or forgiveness in the world for any chick that had the nerve to creep with her man.

The Bryant love child triangle, as gossip blogs had dubbed it, had dominated social media since the news first broke, and even Tatum had to eventually unplug. She hoped Gya would do the same because it would do her no good to consume all the opinions and commentary, many of which were advising Gya to take her money and run since it was now public knowledge that she and Bryant had no prenuptial agreement.

Tatum met up with Kelsea and Ariana at the gym, after which they spent time in the sauna before heading to a restaurant for a light and healthy lunch.

"I really needed that workout. Between Gya and King, I'm at wit's end with worry," Tatum revealed, picking at a salad.

"What's going on with King?" Ariana asked, taking a bite from a piece of avocado toast.

"He's been really frustrated about not getting much playing time."

Kelsea nodded in understanding. "Hey, I've been there. Rookies and their egos don't understand they're now in the big leagues and must prove themselves all over again."

"The frequent traveling schedule is already getting to him. He's also feeling insecure about rookie LA Laker Xavier Malone who is having a great season so far. King was LA's media darling while at UCLA, but now all the hype and focus is on Xavier," Tatum said.

Ariana waved a manicured hand in dismissal. "I've seen lots of players come into the league and start off strong only to choke down the line. Tell King to not despise small beginnings. Slow starters usually emerge to be the stars."

"Well, I'm sure you two have heard about the ongoing problems he's having with Wesley Johnson," Tatum continued.

"Yeah. Antoine has mentioned that since the fight they still have some rather heated arguments during practice and play rather aggressively," Kelsea admitted.

"I don't understand what Wesley's problem is with King. King told me they nearly came to blows again during practice last week," Tatum said.

"Wesley has always been a bonafide jerk if you ask me. It's like I said before, he feels threatened by King because he sees his potential. Be sure to steer clear of him, Tatum, because he's tried to come on to me before," Ariana said.

"Knowing full well you're married to his teammate? Some people have no shame. Reminds me of what Gya is dealing with now. She really considered this Christal person a friend, and she said nothing about her cousin sleeping with Bryant."

"Believe it or not, what she did is not uncommon. It's a lot of WAGs who will smile in your face and then try to hook their friends or family members up with your man. I can say you don't have to worry about that with me and Ariana. I'm hoping we can trust you as well," Kelsea said.

"Girl, I don't even get down like that," Tatum said.

She was so glad to have Kelsea and Ariana in her life. They were really helping her adjust to New York and a life within the spotlight. She liked that she could be authentic and transparent with them, as they understood the ins and outs of such a fast-paced lifestyle, which could be overwhelming at times.

"Has King talked anymore about marriage?" Kelsea asked.

Tatum shook her head. "He's been far too busy."

"Well, look, start putting the pressure on, Tay. Aim for a wedding next summer during the offseason. And actually, I agree with your mom: Getting pregnant will speed up the process," Ariana said only half-joking.

"Nah, don't sell yourself short, Tatum. You're worthy of a ring first," Kelsea spoke up. "And please don't let King string you along. You don't want to end up a five- or ten-year fiancée like so many of these other WAGs."

Back at home later that evening, Tatum was on the phone with her mother discussing Gya and Bryant's current predicament.

"She's taking this really hard, Mom. Not that I blame her. And I don't understand why God would allow something like this to happen to Gya after she's been so faithful. She's started this whole organization to glorify Him only to end up looking like a fool to the masses."

"I understand her being upset, but she needs to suck it up and get over it eventually. Besides, she's not the first woman to be cheated on. Women married to guys with an average nine-to-five deal with adultery. She'd be a fool to divorce him if you ask me."

"But Mom, what about the side baby? That's not something I could overlook."

"It doesn't matter, Tatum. She's in the better position than that silly young broad Bryant was dumb enough to knock up. So long as he fulfills his financial obligation, the baby doesn't have to be a part of their lives. Hell, your father generally did the same thing."

"Exactly, and it had a horrible effect on me. I don't think Bryant should turn his back on this child. It's just as important as the one Gya is carrying and didn't ask to be conceived. If Gya can't accept the child, then maybe it's best she divorces him. It's not fair that the child is neglected because of the selfish act of its parents," Tatum said.

"*Humph,* then let's see if Gya is as holy as she proclaims. Let's see if she's willing to forgive and forget. Didn't I tell you that holiness façade wouldn't last long? God has a way of humbling people and knocking them off their high horse. As for you, just make sure you're stashing away some money for a rainy day. Since you won't take my advice and get pregnant yourself then at least find some way toward securing your financial future."

Not wanting to go down this rabbit hole with her mom again, Tatum bid her a good night and tuned in to King's game on TNT, thinking about how lonely she'd been since he spent most of his time on the road. Those lonesome thoughts quelled her to sleep on the sofa in front of the television.

Chapter Fifteen

Gya was growing tired of awakening with red puffy eyes, and she knew that hardly eating anything was not good for the child forming inside of her. She finally decided to snap out of her pity party and get herself together. Bryant was away on a road trip to Gya's relief. She needed the space, which was why his daily texts and calls went ignored. But she realized something had to give, and she couldn't go on ignoring her husband forever. It was just that the pain hadn't lessened.

Gya's mother informed her that Bryant had phoned to apologize to both her and Gya's father. She told him just as she'd told Gya that it wasn't their place to judge him, and though they were both disappointed in his actions, they understood he was human and prone to mistakes. It angered Gya that Bryant had informed her mother that she'd stayed holed away in their bedroom and was not really eating. Gya had to talk her mother out of flying to Miami after promising her she'd start eating well again and taking care of herself and the baby.

When Bryant arrived home late on Sunday night, he walked in with a sheepish expression. He found Gya nestled on the sofa in front of the television, a blanket covering the lower half of her body. Gya rolled her eyes at the blue Tiffany bag he carried. Bryant silently extended his form of a peace offering to her. In turn, Gya silently took the bag and placed it on the end table next to the sofa, not bothering to look and see what was inside.

"We need to talk," Gya said with such a flatness in her tone that it even surprised her.

"That's what I've been trying to do for the past few days, Gya."

"Bryant, now is not the time to be flip with me," Gya said before taking a deep, long sigh. "If there is any chance of us salvaging this marriage, we need to go to counseling."

Bryant nodded. "I'm open to whatever. I told you I'd do anything to make this right, and I meant that."

"I'm telling you now, we have a long road ahead of us. Right now, I don't know how I'm ever going to trust you again."

Bryant dropped his head, and she could tell her words hurt him. She felt a smidgen of satisfaction, wanting him to hurt just as badly as she did at his betrayal. Bryant placed a kiss on her forehead, feeling her stiffen at his touch. He then went upstairs, and Gya soon heard the shower running.

She peeked inside of the Tiffany's bag, retrieving the box inside. She opened it to find the most beautiful tennis bracelet. But Gya wouldn't let Bryant "buy" his way back into her heart. Sighing, she resolved to pray fervently for the restoration of her marriage.

***

Tatum's mouth dropped, right along with her stomach, as she stared at her gynecologist in disbelief. She attempted to swallow around the huge lump in her throat, forcing her tongue to say the words.

"Ch–Chlamydia?"

"I'm so sorry, Tatum."

Tatum's eyes burned with tears of hurt and anger at the realization that King had given her an STD. Her mind was swirling in all kinds of crazy directions. Who was he creeping with? When did it happen? And why in the hell did he not use protection?

"I'm going to prescribe some oral antibiotics. You should take two a day for two weeks, although your symptoms should start to clear up within a week."

Tatum barely heard her, but she nodded just as her doctor patted her hand and left the examination room so Tatum could get dressed. When she'd made the appointment after experiencing burning while urinating, along with some pelvic discomfort, Tatum had assumed she had a urinary tract infection. Instead, she'd learned that King had been cheating on her, passing along an STD.

She swiped angrily at her hot tears, walking out of the clinic in a daze. Tatum called King immediately but got his voicemail. She left him a rather terse message, instructing him to call her back ASAP.

Once arriving back at their apartment, Tatum took her first round of antibiotics and cried while listening to music on her Apple playlist. She eventually drifted off into a nap. Upon awakening some hours later, she was livid to find that King had not returned her calls. She phoned him once again to no avail and even sent urgent text messages. It was then she realized King was probably aware that she knew he'd infected her and was now avoiding her calls. Tatum began to sob uncontrollably.

Kelsea had invited her and Ariana to a watch party of tonight's game at her home. Tatum was in no mood, but she felt that being around her friends would help take her mind off this waking nightmare that had become her life in the blink of an eye.

Tatum tried to hold her emotions together, but from the moment she walked in and Kelsea gave her a huge smile in greeting, the dam broke, and the flood of tears came bursting forth once again.

Ariana's features were a mask of concern as she led Tatum over to the sofa, and Kelsea came with a bottle of water. The entire sordid tale came from Tatum's lips through hiccups and sobs. Once she'd finished, she watched Ariana and Kelsea exchange glances, then Kelsea sighed.

"So, you've gotten your first STD. Welcome to the WAGs club, girlfriend. You've officially been indoctrinated."

"Kelsea, how can you joke about something like this. Wait—so I take it you've had an STD before too?"

"Yes, and so have I," Ariana spoke up, then she raised her hand. "And before you go judging us—"

Tatum cut her off. "I'm not judging," she assured.

"Listen, it would be nothing we haven't heard before. You know how many fools I was called by my family for staying? But it's funny how their tune changed once Russell threw cash in their direction. Money always seems to make things better, right?" Ariana said.

"Money can't fix this. And now King is avoiding my calls," Tatum said.

"Girl, of course he is. He's probably already been treated for the infection. He knows you know, so he's trying to get an airtight story together or a slew of excuses. Trust me, when he finally talks to you, he will have his own sob story," Kelsea said.

"The question is, what are you gonna do now? Are you gonna leave him behind this or use it to your advantage?" Ariana asked.

"What do you mean?" Tatum asked.

"You have leverage now to get whatever you want. If King loves you as much as you say he does, he'll do anything to make this up to you. Use this to finally get your ring, girl," Ariana said.

"I'm not even sure I still want to marry him. What if he'd passed along HIV? How can I spend the rest of my life with someone who will place my life at risk like that? How hard is it for these stupid men to use protection?" Tatum said. She now understood exactly how Gya felt.

"Tatum, now you're overthinking things. I mean, look at all that you have with King. Are you gonna kick him to the curb and end up marrying some college graduate that's swimming in student loan debt when your life is financially set with King? Pick and choose your battles, Tay. The pros that come with this lifestyle far outweigh the cons. Don't let your emotions cause you to throw it all away. Like Ariana said, play on King's emotions and have him spoil you until he's back in your good graces. Get the ring," Kelsea coached.

"I mean, if you want to play with his head a little, you can act like you're about to pack up and leave. Trust me, he'll be on his best behavior then. Also make him use condoms for a while. Girl, that drove Russell crazy," Ariana said.

"I don't want him anywhere near me," Tatum said, disgusted at the thought of her and King being intimate again anytime soon.

"Well use that too then. Cut him off from sex," Kelsea said.

"He'll just get it from someone else as he's obviously been doing. I feel so...stupid, y'all. There were no signs that he was cheating."

"Besides that burning vajay-jay." Ariana laughed.

"Not funny, Ariana," Tatum said. "Hey, do y'all remember that one woman who was married to that Houston Meteor football player, Gabriel Shephard? He passed along HIV to her."

"Yes. Her name is Sydney. She's now an AIDS advocate," Kelsea said.

"Yeah, well I don't want to end up like her," Tatum reasoned.

"Well, tell King if he places you at risk like that again then you're gone, and you'll sue him," Ariana said. "Bet that would get his attention. Come for his pockets."

Tatum sighed and laid her head back against the sofa, placing her hands against her throbbing temples. "I just don't know."

***

Tatum left Kelsea's house after the start of the third quarter. The Flash were in the lead against the Milwaukee Bucks by twenty points, but Tatum was in no mood to celebrate. Back inside of her apartment, she felt so conflicted. Perhaps going to Kelsea's had been a mistake because both she and Ariana had her second-guessing herself. She felt willing to forgive King and move past this transgression, but she didn't want to become a doormat.

Tatum had been putting it off, but she felt compelled to call Gya. She knew her cousin had her plate full with the Bryant love-child scandal but Gya could actually give Tatum sound advice because she was experiencing the same betrayal.

Gya was silent on the other end of the line as Tatum spilled the entire ordeal.

"Kelsea and Ariana are telling me to suck it up and stay, but I don't know if that's the best thing."

"Because it's not, Tay. You need to leave King."

Tatum blinked in surprise at the adamance in Gya's tone. "So I should pack my bags just like that? Need I point out you're not leaving Bryant?"

"Bryant and I are *married*, Tatum. You have no official ties to King, so it shouldn't be that difficult."

"What about love, Gya?"

"Well, in your case, that's not going to be enough."

"What about *your* case? Is it enough for you and Bryant?"

"This isn't about us, Tatum. Look, what do you want exactly? You weren't feeling your friends telling you to stay, and now that I'm advising you to leave, you aren't feeling that either. So what in the hell do you want? And if you have everything figured out, then why in the hell did you call me?"

"Yeah, I'm realizing that was a mistake. And since I know you're dealing with a lot of stress, I won't check you for your tone or your attitude. This whole thing with Bryant has really done a number on your personality if you're going around cursing at people now." Tatum said.

"Well, again, *you* called me."

"Yeah, but I didn't expect to receive all of the hypocrisy."

"Bryant didn't give me an STD."

"He *could* have, and if you ask me, having a baby with another woman is far worse. After the antibiotics, I'll be cured, but you have a lingering reminder of Bryant's infidelity on your hands. I called you because I felt like you could relate to what I was going through and would give me some sound advice, but I see you're being your usual judgmental self. Gya, did you ever stop to think that maybe God allowed this situation to happen to humble you?"

"And maybe you got an STD because it's God's way of showing you that He doesn't approve of you shacking up," Gya shot back.

"You know what Gya, go to hell," Tatum yelled, hanging up on her cousin.

Her chest heaved in anger. When her cell phone rang, she snatched it up without bothering to look at the caller ID.

"And don't even try coming at me with your God-filled apologies."

"Apologies for what?" King asked.

Tatum blinked in confusion. Glancing at her phone, she saw King's name and photo.

"Oh, my fault. I thought you were Gya. But yes, you have some apologizing and explaining to do yourself, so don't even try to sit up here playing dumb."

"You're really tripping on me not returning your calls all day? You know how preoccupied I get on game days."

"That's no reason to ignore my calls, King, especially concerning something as serious as an STD. You know good and well that's why you were really avoiding my calls."

"Whoa, what? Who has an STD?"

"King, stop. You gave me chlamydia, and I know you've been burning too."

"You have chlamydia?"

"So you really gonna sit up here and play games?"

"Who gave it to you?"

"King, you know damn good and well I haven't been unfaithful to you."

"I don't know anything. As much as you run the streets with Ariana and Kelsea, there's no telling what the three of you are into."

"Oh, so I passed it along to you?" Tatum couldn't help but laugh at his gall.

"You know you're doing the exact same thing you did on the night of the Bruins championship—making everything about you. We pulled off one helluva win, and I'm the top scorer for tonight's game. Given all the crap I had to take from Wesley, I'd think you'd be celebrating with me, but instead you tell me you've given me an STD."

"King, stop this. You know I haven't cheated on you. How can you sit here and turn this around on me?"

"Look, I can't believe this. We'll talk when I get home." King hung up.

Tatum stood staring at the phone in disbelief. Instead of apologizing for his cheating and deceit, he'd gaslighted her. She couldn't believe he could behave in such a conniving and manipulative manner.

Mulling over how she was now at odds with both her cousin and her man, Tatum walked into the bathroom and opened the medicine cabinet to take her second dose of antibiotics. She glanced at the other prescription pill bottles belonging to King that lined the medicine cabinet—medications prescribed for various minor injuries he'd sustained. As tears poured down her cheeks, Tatum contemplated opening the bottles and taking all the pills, ending everything. She just wanted this pain to go away.

Chapter Sixteen

"Mercedes is dropping the paternity suit," Bryant said as he stood gazing at Gya from the doorway of their bedroom.

Gya looked up from the daily prayer devotional she was reading. "Oh really? Why?"

"Because she knows there is no truth to it, Gya, just like I told you all along. I wished you'd had as much faith in me as you do in God."

Gya laughed and looked at him as if he were pathetic. "Are you serious? Bryant, I did put faith in you only for you to turn around and be unfaithful to me. Dropped paternity suit or not, the fact remains you cheated on me. Mercedes recanting doesn't erase that. Is she even pregnant?"

"I don't know and don't care. All I'm concerned about is that it's not mine. I want to put all this past us and move forward."

Gya was quiet and thoughtful for a moment, then she sighed. "Okay. I'm willing to do that, and remember, we have our first counseling appointment next week. Gosh, I can't believe we've already come to this point." Gya felt the onslaught of tears emerging again but forced them not to drop. She was tired of crying—of the days and nights filled with sobs.

"I know I messed up. Big time. And I'm willing to do whatever I need to make it right, so if you want counseling, that's what we'll take on. I love you, Gya. I mean that and always will. Don't forget it."

With one last longing gaze in her direction, he turned and left. Gya heard the garage door opening as he prepared to go to team practice.

Gya closed her devotional and grabbed her cell phone and iPad. She walked into her home office and sat in front of her computer with her other devices, setting each of them to livestream from her various social media platforms. Adjusting her ring light to the correct amount of brightness, she smiled at her virtual audience.

"Good morning, everyone. I wanted to come on briefly and share a few things with you. First, the paternity suit against my husband has been dropped. He and I are resolving to move forward from this trial. The enemy has not been successful in tearing my marriage apart. Bryant and I will undergo marital counseling, and we are seeking your prayers for restoration of trust within our marriage. I am going to take a hiatus from Well Worth the Wait while I focus on repairing the damage to my relationship. I cannot pour from an empty cup. I can't minister effectively amid so much pain and confusion. Despite his faults and shortcomings, I still love Bryant dearly. I know God hates divorce, so that is not an option I am willing to seek. God bless you, and I love you all. Thank you."

Gya signed off and exhaled long and hard, silently praying for God's grace to shepherd her through the rest of the journey toward healing and forgiveness.

***

Tatum logged off from Gya's livestream. She was still rather angry at her cousin but couldn't help but admire her resiliency and courage. Tatum then grew filled with bitterness as she thought about King's cowardly act. He had yet to return to their apartment, and Tatum knew his disappearing act meant he was laid up with some other woman once again. She couldn't take the disrespect anymore and knew she had a tough decision to make, but she needed wise counsel first. She picked up the phone and called her aunt Pam.

"Auntie, I'm so sorry to bother you. I know your plate is full with Gya and her marital issues."

"Tatum, you know how much I love you, and you're never a burden on me. Now what's going on?" Pam encouraged.

Tatum filled her in on all that transpired with King and the STD. She ended with her argument with Gya concerning how to handle the situation.

"Gya's judgment is clouded by pain and misery right now, which is why she snapped on you. That's why I'm glad she's taking a break from that women's ministry to try and heal. As for you, no one can tell you what decisions to make concerning your relationship other than you. Have you prayed on this, sweetheart?"

"Yes, and I feel God is telling me to pack my things and leave."

"Well, you know God would never lead you wrong. So, what's stopping you?"

"It's so hard, auntie. I love King so much and don't want to lose him."

"But is staying with him worth losing yourself? Tatum, what happened to that beautiful and confident cheerleader who had so many goals and ambitions

83

when she first came to UCLA? You know, God often uses situations to garner our attention, even with Gya. You know how much I love my daughter, but she became a bit too overzealous with this whole Well Worth the Wait movement. She didn't even realize her ego got huge and she was caught up in the adoration of all those impressionable young women across the world who want what she has—the idea of a glamorous marriage. God used this present test to get her to slow down and examine her ways. And He's probably doing the same for you."

"But what if King moves on and finds someone else?"

"I know it will hurt, but it won't be the end of the world, Tatum. You can re-enroll in school and possibly meet someone else as well. What if King is not the man God has for you? You could be blocking your blessings by remaining in a dead-end relationship. If King stays in your life, you can't make room for anyone else. Baby, trust me, the worst thing you can do is wake up one day and realize you wasted the best years of your life on a man and a relationship that isn't going anywhere. I mean it's one thing if King was remorseful and truly apologetic for his actions, but him lying and trying to blame you for this situation displays that he doesn't truly love and care for you as he may have claimed. You have King on the same pedestal most of the world has him on, and he's starting to believe his own hype obviously. Always remember you're just as much of a prize. He should cherish you as much as you cherish being with him."

"I understand everything you're saying, auntie. And as much as I love King, I can't put up or tolerate blatant disrespect. That's why I wanted to call you. I haven't even told my mom about this because she'd only encourage me to stay. She's so blinded by King and his newfound fame and money. I don't want to be a slave to that."

"So, Tatum, it sounds like you know exactly what you need to do."

"You're right." Tatum sighed. "And I'm going to do it. I'm leaving."

"I'm always here if you need anything. Would you like to stay with me, or do you want to return to your mother's?"

"I'm going to go back to my mom's. By the time I get there, it will be too late for her to talk me out of it. She'll fuss a bit, but I know eventually she'll accept my decision to walk away."

"Okay, well I love you, niecey, and again, don't hesitate to call me for anything else."

Tatum told her aunt that she loved her too and went to start packing her things.

85

Chapter Seventeen

"My career entails me being in the spotlight, so when I come home to a space that is supposed to be a safe sanctuary, I don't want to have to deal with a camera in my face," Bryant said, a solemn expression on his face as he and Gya sat on a loveseat within the therapist's office.

Gya immediately grew defensive. "There you go again, blaming my ministry for the breakdown of this marriage. And since we're being totally honest here, my vlogging is also a way to pass the time when you're on the road for a good majority of the month, or would you rather I engage in my own infidelity to keep myself preoccupied?"

Bryant's expression went from solemn to one of suppressed rage at the thought of Gya creeping on him. The therapist, Stephanie Coles, noticed his change in demeanor as well and quickly intervened before things could grow heated.

"Gya, one of the points of these sessions is honesty. Bryant has done that. You must take his thoughts and feelings into consideration without growing upset," Dr. Coles pointed out.

"Let's talk about what he can change then. How about not sleeping around? Since we're being honest and all." Gya said.

"See, Dr. Coles it's been like this ever since she found out about the affair—a merry-go-round. We can't make progress if she continues to keep throwing my mistake up in my face."

"Don't talk about me as if I'm not sitting right here, Bryant." Gya said, rubbing her belly and hoping that her annoyance and frustration wasn't upsetting their unborn child.

Bryant just sighed.

"Bryant, I understand your frustration, but you have to realize your betrayal of Gya is not going to disappear because you're ready to move on. You must understand the depth of her hurt and pain. As much as you don't want to hear this, you're going to have to be patient as she works through it all," Dr. Coles said.

She then turned to Gya. "Gya, you've told me you've decided to remain in the marriage. To do that, you have to move forward. You must make an effort to not rehash the mistake. Since our session is ending, I want to give you both an assignment to work on this week. Until our next session, I want you to not mention the affair. Neither of you. Not once."

"Oh, trust, doc, you don't have to worry about me mentioning it," Bryant assured.

"Oh, of course you wouldn't," Gya said snidely.

"Use this week to get back to the basics. I want you to think about when you first met. Try to recapture the essence of that time. Gya, do you think you can do that?"

"All I can do is try," Gya said softly.

***

And try she did.

Gya had to admit that by the middle of the week, the assignment the therapist challenged them to complete was effective. Biting her tongue was a struggle in the beginning, but Gya soon grew hopeful that her marriage could be salvaged.

She found herself humming the Jonathan McReynolds song "Grace" as she showered in preparation for her and Bryant to go out and enjoy an afternoon lunch. Gya was just rinsing the last suds from her body when she noticed bleeding from her vagina. She gasped in panic, realizing this was a sign of an impending miscarriage.

"Bryant," she managed to croak out just as a cramp hit her abdomen.

Hearing the distress in his wife's voice, Bryant rushed into the bathroom to find her doubled over, her hand glistening with blood.

"Oh God, please don't let me lose this baby," she said, sobbing.

Bryant immediately phoned for an ambulance while helping Gya get cleaned up and dried off, placing a towel over her vagina to try to stop the bleeding. Paramedics soon arrived and transported her to the University of Miami hospital with Bryant trailing in his vehicle.

Gya's fears were confirmed as the doctors sadly informed her that the fetus was no longer viable. She sobbed uncontrollably as the doctor informed her of her options. She could wait for the fetus to pass naturally or have a D&C performed. Gya was informed that if she chose the first option, medication would be prescribed to help the contents of her uterus to be expelled within forty-eight hours. Gya didn't want to endure any further agony and decided on the D&C. She was placed under anesthesia and the operation was performed.

***

When Tatum learned of Gya's miscarriage, she accompanied her aunt Pam to Miami to visit her cousin who'd been placed on bedrest to recover.

Tatum greeted Bryant warmly, but she noticed he avoided her and Pam's eyes. Tatum figured he was embarrassed and experiencing a lot of guilt about everything that had transpired. But she wasn't there to point fingers or judge. She just wanted to be a source of support for Gya, their past argument long forgotten as far as she was concerned. But Tatum couldn't help but wish that King displayed the same form of humility for his own transgressions.

As soon as Tatum and her mother entered her bedroom, Gya teared up once again. Without hesitation, Tatum went to envelop her cousin in the deepest and longest hug.

"I'm so sorry about how I spoke to you during our last conversation. Maybe that's why this has happened to me," Gya lamented.

"Girl, now you know better than that. You are not being punished for anything," Tatum soothed.

"I agree, Gya. Please don't blame yourself," Pam chimed in.

"But, Mom, didn't you say it yourself? I was too prideful and haughty, and maybe God is using this miscarriage as a way of humbling me," Gya continued to bemoan. "I mean, everything was starting to look up again. Bryant and I were in a much better space, and then this happens. I feel like God is punishing me for something."

"Gya, we may never understand the ways of God, but I know I will forever trust Him, and deep down you feel the same. I know your faith in God can never be shaken, and so does the enemy. The devil keeps trying to get you to break. You continue to stand strong and firm. Never lose faith," Pam encouraged.

They spent the day with Gya, praying and ordering in food. Pam had to practically force Gya to eat, telling her she needed to get her strength back up. Gya admitted she hadn't had much of an appetite since losing the baby.

"I know this sounds cliché, but you and Bryant can always try again," Pam said.

"The thought of having sex with Bryant again is the furthest thing from my mind right now. Honestly, I don't want him anywhere near me," Gya admitted. "We were making such good progress with the therapist. Now I feel like we're right back to square one. He's been trying to be so overly attentive since I came home from the hospital, but his constant hovering is getting on my nerves. I feel like he's only doing it out of guilt, and sadly enough, I do blame him." Gya's voice trailed off with those last words.

That evening, Tatum checked into a hotel, declining Gya's invite to stay over at her home, as they had plenty of room. Tatum insisted on not crowding her and Bryant. Pam stayed out in the guesthouse.

The following day, Tatum returned to Houston, and she received a phone call from Kelsea. As promised, both she and Ariana kept in touch with Tatum since her split from King.

"I hate to be the bearer of bad news, but since you've left, King has been seen with different women, both around NYC and when he's on road trips. But Antoine has told me he thinks King is just using them to fill the void you left, and I agree. He really misses you, Tatum, but his pride won't let him reach out and ask you to come back. Antoine said he was livid when he finally returned to the apartment and found you gone."

"I think that was more so his ego in action. He couldn't believe I had the gall to leave him," Tatum said.

"Well, Ariana and I miss you too. Do you think once the dust settles, you'll consider giving him another chance? Look, I'm gonna be real: Ariana is cool and all, but I'm tired of seeing our men fall into the arms of 'the others' if you know what I mean. King hasn't been discriminatory when it comes to the women he's been seen with lately. There's this one blond, blue-eyed chick that he's been seen with most frequently. I wish you would consider taking him back before blondie tries to make things official with him."

Tatum's heart was breaking with each word Kelsea spoke. The fact that King was already trying to replace her was unbearable.

"I'm big on building generational wealth, and I'm tired of seeing black money transferred to other ethnicities. Black women are just as deserving of lavish lifestyles. Don't you agree?"

"Have you been talking to my mother?" Tatum joked to lighten the mood and her heart.

Kelsea laughed. "Just think about what I said."

"But Kelsea, that's just it. King has not reached out to me. It's obvious he wants to move on."

"I feel his silence is due to embarrassment. He knows he messed up royally by giving you the STD. Look, just take a little more time, but I think you should try to get back with him before Christmas. Let him buy you loads of gifts to make up for his indiscretion. It'll be a jolly Christmas indeed for you, girl." Kelsea laughed again.

Once hanging up, Tatum reflected on her awkward return to Houston, having to field questions from friends and family about King's whereabouts. Tatum found it hard to admit to others that things hadn't worked out between them. But since being back home, Tatum connected with her old church and was attending services regularly again, the one bright spot within this entire ordeal. Tatum enjoyed re-establishing her relationship with God, and she was seeking Him daily for direction on what to do with the rest of her life. But she was really praying that God would lead her back to King.

Chapter Eighteen

Tatum was dreading the upcoming holiday season, her first in a long time without King at her side. It didn't help matters that the Flash had a game against the Houston Asteroids on the Wednesday evening before Thanksgiving. King's entire family would be in attendance, and his mother, Michelle, had even invited Tatum to their Thanksgiving celebration at their home in Memphis the following day, but Tatum politely declined. It warmed her heart that Michelle was still welcoming her into their home, but Tatum didn't want to risk seeing King with some new girl. She watched the game, and the Flash put a hurting on the Asteroids. But Tatum turned the channel right before King's post-game interview. She realized watching the game had been a mistake because it further dampened her mood. Seeing his handsome face was another dagger to her heart.

Gya was in town for Thanksgiving, and Pam hosted a huge Thanksgiving spread at their home. Since Vanessa would be spending the holiday with some new man she'd been seeing, Tatum decided to spend Thanksgiving with her aunt and cousins. Bryant wouldn't be present since the Waves had a game scheduled against the Pittsburgh Steelers on that afternoon.

"What made you decide to spend Thanksgiving here in Houston instead of traveling to Pittsburgh?" Tatum asked Gya as they piled their plates with the delicious spread of food Pam had catered.

"Believe it or not, Bryant and I still aren't really talking. Well, I'm not talking to him. We've been in separate beds since the miscarriage."

"Wow. Things are still that bad?"

"I fell into a deep depression after you and Mom left Miami. I hardly ate or got out of bed. I didn't want Bryant anywhere near me. I could sense his hurt and frustration, but I just needed my space. I realize it may be selfish because the miscarriage affected him too. And to be honest, I'm still not at one hundred percent."

"Well, I'm glad you seemed to pull yourself out of your funk enough to come to Houston. It's great seeing you." Before Tatum could say anything further, they were interrupted by their cousin Jasmin.

"Tatum, now that King is out of the picture, will you be re-enrolling in school?" she nosily asked.

"That's what I'd like to know too," Jasmin's mother, Angela, butted in. "And how are you doing, Gya? I brought you some literature on healing from miscarriages and some options you and Bryant can take toward conceiving again."

Gya frowned. "What do you mean options?"

"I just assumed maybe the miscarriage was brought on by pregnancy complications—you know, underlying fertility issues."

"I never thought that, Mom. It's obvious the stress from Bryant's cheating caused her to miscarry," Jasmin stated.

"You know what, I'm not going to have this conversation with the two of you. With all due respect, I find you both rather intrusive and insensitive right now," Gya said.

Angela raised her hands in defense. "You're right, niece, and we apologize. I just thought that as family we could candidly discuss these things. I didn't mean to offend."

An awkward silence ensued and was soon replaced by the sounds of silverware clinking against plates as everyone focused on their food.

"As far as me re-enrolling in school, I haven't decided yet," Tatum spoke up. Not that she owed them any explanation, but she did want to deflect the attention away from Gya and her marital issues.

"Well, you need to decide something quick now that your meal ticket has left the building. What made you decide to finally call it quits? Let me guess: He cheated too, right?" Jasmin prodded. "I for one am glad I never tried to take up with an athlete. Not worth the headache."

"Jasmin, I've always told you that you could do so much better. I can't wait until you bring home a fellow doctor," Angela said.

Chalking her aunt and cousin up to a lost cause, Tatum focused on her plate and enjoyed the rest of her meal.

After eating and fellowship, most of the family moved into the den to tune in to the Waves game against the Steelers. Mouths and hearts dropped when Bryant went down right before halftime. The Waves medical staff and other team personnel rushed onto the field to tend to their fallen player.

Gya looked on, wringing her hands in worry. "C'mon, baby. Get up," she murmured.

Groans ensued as a stretcher was wheeled onto the field, alerting all present that Bryant's injury was serious.

Gya grabbed her phone as he was wheeled off the field, hoping to reach the athletic trainer so he could give her a play-by-play of what was going on with Bryant, but her call went to voicemail. Gya frantically kept trying to reach other team personnel.

"*Humph*. Serves him right if you ask me. This is comeuppance for how he's treated my niece." Angela stated.

Gya whirled around and turned to glare at her aunt. "Are you serious right now?"

"Angela, you're out of line," Pam spoke up. "I won't have this foolishness in my home."

"But Mom is right. The Bible does state that you reap what you sow. Maybe this is the price Bryant has to pay for his infidelity. Let's just pray that God has mercy on him and his injury isn't too serious or career-ending," Jasmin chimed in.

"You know what, I'm headed to Pittsburgh. Let me get out of here before I say something I'll regret," Gya said.

"Baby, don't go to Pittsburgh," Gya's father said. "I'm sure they'll be sending Bryant home later tonight or early tomorrow morning depending on if he needs to be hospitalized. Why don't you fly back to Miami and wait for him?"

"Dad, I want to be wherever my husband is. I can't wait until tomorrow to see him if that's the case. I need to know that he's alright," Gya responded.

"Do you need me to go with you?" Tatum offered.

"Tatum, don't be dramatic. It's more than likely some knee injury. He wasn't shot," Angela said.

Tatum ignored her overbearing aunt, restraining from rolling her eyes.

"No, cousin, you've flown out to attend to me enough already in the past few months. Mom, Dad, I'll let you know if I need you to fly in," Gya said as she went to gather her things.

***

Gya managed to reach someone from team personnel who informed her that Bryant was under observation and being x-rayed. They assured her he would be flown back to Miami that night, so she decided to fly home instead.

Tatum returned home to an empty house, as Vanessa was still across town spending the Thanksgiving holiday at the home of her new guy friend. The silence triggered thoughts about King. She wondered what he and his family were doing and if he'd brought a date over. Strolling into the kitchen, Tatum removed an opened bottle of wine that belonged to Vanessa from the refrigerator. After two glasses, she went into her room and laid across the bed fully clothed, the wine lulling her to sleep.

Tatum felt herself being shoved awake. She groggily looked around into the darkness of the room, the only light coming from the opened door. She saw her mother's form standing over her. Vanessa appeared excited.

"Tatum, King is here to see you."

This caused Tatum to be more alert. Was she dreaming?

Just as Tatum sat up, she saw King's tall form filling her doorway. He turned on the bedroom light, and Tatum squinted against the sudden brightness.

"Dang, girl. You look wasted," King joked.

"I'll leave you two alone to catch up," Vanessa said.

She gave Tatum a wink and a thumbs up as she closed the bedroom door behind her.

King came and sat next to her on the bed. Tatum's heart leaped at his nearness, and as she inhaled the alluring scent of his cologne. She was elated to see him but told herself to play it cool.

King ran his fingers through strands of Tatum's hair. "I was disappointed not to see you at my game last night," he revealed.

"Did you really expect me to show up?"

"I've missed you a lot, Tatum. Look, I'm sorry. It was foul of me to blame you for the STD. I apologize for putting your health at risk. Honestly, I freaked out when I tested positive. I didn't know what to do and just decided to wait it out and hope you weren't infected. That's why I behaved the way I did. What I feared the most happened, and that was losing you."

Tatum felt herself melting at his words and then wanted to kick herself for always being so quick to cave in to him. Why did he have such a hold over her? Did this mean they were soul mates? Would their hearts forever be intertwined? It sure felt like it to Tatum because it seemed like no matter how wrong or badly King treated her, she just couldn't stay away or stay mad at him for long.

"Well, it seems like it didn't take you long to replace me. I've heard about the girls you've been with since I've been gone."

"Baby, they were just time fillers. It's you that has my heart, and I want to prove it."

Tatum's heart nearly dropped out of her chest as King removed a small black box from his pocket. Her eyes ballooned as he got down on one knee.

"Tatum, will you marry me?"

They were interrupted by a loud scream from Vanessa, who'd obviously been standing outside the door.

"Well, it sounds like I have one vote of approval." King laughed.

Tears welled up in Tatum's eyes, and she wrapped her arms around King, kissing him long and hard.

"So, I take it that's a yes?" he teased.

"Yes, baby. I want to spend forever with you," Tatum replied through her tears.

King grinned and slid the princess-cut diamond ring upon her finger.

"You can come in now, Mama, with your nosy self," Tatum said.

That was all the encouragement Vanessa needed to burst into the room and pull King into a huge bear hug.

"My son-in-law-to-be. I can't wait to start planning this wedding."

"C'mon, Tay. Let's call my folks and announce the good news," King said. "I left my family's Thanksgiving celebration to fly here and beg you to come back to me."

"King, I want you to know I'm accepting this ring under the condition of respect and fidelity. Nothing like this STD incident can ever happen again. No outside babies or paternity suits or I'm gone for good. Also, there will not be a long engagement. We need to be married by next summer. Are we clear?"

"Crystal clear, baby," King said, grabbing her newly adorned ring finger and bringing it to his lips for a soft, tender kiss.

King's mother was ecstatic when they called her with the news. Vanessa brought out more wine for a toast to their future nuptials, and Tatum's heart was full. She felt God not only heard her prayers but exceeded her expectations, blessing her with marriage. Her holiday season had gone from dismal to merry again in the blink of an eye, displaying that he was definitely a God of "suddenly" and could change a situation around in an instant.

Tatum decided to return to New York with King the following day. He would sleep in their guest bedroom, and they'd head to the airport first thing in the morning. Tatum was just about to turn in for the night, but she wanted to make sure King had enough blankets. She walked to the guest room and was about to knock when she heard King talking to his father, Jacoby. His phone seemed to be on speaker or perhaps FaceTime because Tatum could hear Jacoby's voice clearly.

"I personally think the both of you are a bit too young for all of this marriage talk. On the other hand, a family man image will be good for future endorsement opportunities. You just be sure she signs a prenup before you two walk down the aisle—an ironclad one," Jacoby said.

Tatum held her breath, waiting for King to say something in opposition to his father's suggestion, but all she heard was King saying okay in agreement and then telling his father he was tired and turning in for the night.

Tatum moved away from the door and returned to her bedroom, trying to gather her bearings and not allow what she'd overheard to dampen her spirits. King had always been a sucker when it came to standing up to his father. Tatum resolved that she wouldn't allow Jacoby and his territorial ways over his son to drive a wedge between their relationship. She'd even sign the stupid prenup as proof that she truly loved King and wasn't at his side for his riches and fame.

Chapter Nineteen

Bryant suffered a knee injury that was more serious than everyone thought. Serious enough to sideline him for the remainder of the season.

From the moment he'd returned to Miami, he was in low spirits. Gya put all past differences aside and was determined to nurse her husband back to health.

"You know I now have no chance of being voted as Rookie of the Year. The Waves' record is mediocre at best this season, and even if we make it to the playoffs, I really don't see the team advancing as far as the conference finals, much less the Super Bowl," he lamented to Gya.

Gya softly rubbed his arm as they nestled side by side together in bed. "You're still a winner in my book. Don't even worry yourself with all of that right now. Just focus on rehabbing that knee so you can bounce back better and stronger for your sophomore season."

Bryant grabbed her hand, which was adorned by her wedding ring, bringing it to his lips for a gentle kiss. "I don't deserve you."

Gya placed a kiss upon his forehead. "You're right. You don't," she said with a laugh.

Bryant's features grew serious. "Gya, I honestly think this sidelining injury is God's punishment for my infidelity."

"Bryant, we're not going to rehash that, okay? You know that God makes all things work together for good, so a blessing will emerge from this."

He squeezed her hand. "Perhaps it's the full restoration of our marriage. I'll have a lot more time to spend with you now, and once my knee is fully healed, we can work on making another baby. But in the meantime, why don't we try another alternative to bring a little spice to the bedroom?" Bryant said with a mischievous wiggling of his eyebrows.

"And what might that be?" Gya asked, looking a bit skeptical.

With a grin Bryant grabbed his cell phone, clicking open his iTunes app. He then laughed when the opening melody to SWV's song "Downtown" began to play.

Gya playfully mushed his head. "Boy, now see, you've lost your mind. You sure you didn't bump your head when you took that hit?"

"C'mon, baby. You're not down—no pun intended?"

"*Ummm,* no. You know I don't believe in oral sex. I've always viewed it as filthy and something that's connected to prostitution and those slutty groupie types," Gya said, wrinkling her nose in distaste.

"Gya, doesn't the Bible state that the marriage bed is undefiled?"

"I'm sure that is not what God had in mind."

Bryant groaned. "So what am I supposed to do for the next few weeks while my knee is healing? I mean you've been holding out on me for a while now, baby. I'm backed up over here."

"Don't be gross," Gya said while biting back the urge to retort that her bedroom boycott was his fault from the very beginning. She remembered they were supposed to be moving forward.

"Gya, stop being so prudish. We're married, and it's like I said before, you're always quick to toss around scriptures but turn a blind eye to certain ones that don't fit your agenda."

"Agenda? Wait a minute. Are you calling me a hypocrite?"

"Look, Gya, we are both grown. Now that we're married, I can expect certain things from my wife."

"So, I'm a robot now, Bryant?"

"You know what, just forget it. I can already see we're headed toward another argument. Let's just drop the whole thing, okay?" Bryant nestled his head into his pillow, a sign he was about to take a nap.

Sighing, Gya got up and left the bedroom, but their conversation continued to replay in her head. Bryant had never pressured her concerning oral sex before. She couldn't help but wonder if Mercedes performed it on him during their tryst. Gya's heart twisted in jealousy at the thought of some other woman being able to please and satisfy her husband. And what if Gya never succumbed to his request? Would he seek out another groupie to fulfill his desires?

***

Tatum's eyes lit up in excitement as the Flash City Dancers entered the private event room of Del Frisco's Steakhouse carrying bottles of Dom Perignon with fiery sparklers attached. Her family and friends stood as her beautiful three-tiered cake was rolled out by the waitstaff, and they then begin to sing Happy Birthday.

A teary-eyed Tatum leaned forward once they were done, blowing out her twenty-two candles. She then turned to King who was standing at her side, giving him a hug and a kiss for funding such a wonderful birthday celebration on her behalf.

Ever since their reconciliation, Tatum had felt truly blessed and hopeful about their future. The wedding was set for the following year on Fourth of July weekend. Tatum filled most of her days with the planning, with Vanessa assisting through phone calls and FaceTime.

"You and King look so happy tonight," Kelsea remarked as everyone prepared to leave.

"We are, girl. He's done a one-eighty, and I think we are going to be okay. I'm glad all the mess and drama is behind us." Tatum beamed.

"I'm looking forward to the wedding. You be sure and hold him to that date too. Don't let him try to put it off," Kelsea advised. She then slid Tatum a card.

Tatum looked at it and frowned. "A private investigator, Kelsea?"

"Just keep it on hand as a little insurance. Many of the Flash wives use this woman. She's good and thorough," Kelsea said.

She bid Tatum good night, and she and her husband, Antoine, left the restaurant.

Tatum went to the restroom, and when she exited, Wesley Johnson was just coming out of the men's restroom. Invites for her birthday celebration had been extended to the entire Flash team, and she was surprised that Wesley had shown up, given the tension that lingered between him and King. Tatum gave him a brief smile and went to walk past him, but he blocked her path.

"Can I ask you something? Why does a beautiful woman like yourself put up with someone like King?" Wesley moved in toward her, draping an arm around her shoulder.

"Excuse me? Wesley, can you please move? You're violating my personal space. I don't want any mess tonight."

Wesley removed his arm and raised his hands in a gesture of innocence. "I'm not trying to ruin your birthday, and I mean no disrespect. A woman like you deserves the utmost respect. Baby girl, you can't be in love with a man who's more in love with himself."

"Look, Wesley, back off, okay? My relationship with King is none of your business," Tatum snapped, now regretting having invited this fool.

"When you get fed up, give me a call so I can show you how a woman is supposed to be treated," Wesley said with a chuckle.

Tatum gazed after him, her chest heaving and nostrils flaring in anger. But his words gave her pause. She wondered if Wesley was slyly insinuating that King was still being unfaithful. Tatum opened her purse and fingered the card Kelsea had given her. Sighing, she went to go find her family so they could leave the restaurant. She debated telling King about the conversation with Wesley, but King would only lose his temper and cause a scene. Not wanting to put any further damper on her birthday celebration, Tatum decided to put the exchange out of her mind. As soon as she got home, she was going to trash the private investigator card. Tatum resolved to trust her man.

Chapter Twenty

With King away on a road trip, Tatum found herself alone in their apartment, reflecting over her birthday celebration while thumbing through bridal magazines. Her heart warmed every time she thought of the effort King had put into making her birthday amazing and special.

Tatum was jolted from her thoughts by the sound of the doorbell. She frowned. All guests had to be announced by the front lobby concierge before being sent up. Tatum had not received any notice of a visitor. She then began to smile. It was probably some post-birthday surprise delivery arranged by King.

But when Tatum looked through the peephole, she saw a tall, attractive woman standing in front of the door, her black and Asian features masked in impatience. Tatum rolled her eyes. Did some fan manage to sneak past building security and make her way to their apartment?

"Can I help you?" Tatum asked upon opening the door, hoping the tone in her voice would let this unwelcome visitor know she wasn't in the mood for nonsense.

"Where King at?"

"Excuse me? You don't show up at my door asking for my man. And furthermore, I'm sure he wouldn't appreciate some random fan showing up to his home. Now leave before I call security," Tatum said, about to slam the door in her face.

The woman grabbed the door. "I can assure you King had no complaints about me the other night," she said. Tatum watched as she pulled a red thong from her purse and flung it at Tatum. "Here, I forgot to leave him with a keepsake. It's torn because King is so impatient. He wanted to get right down to business and ripped my thong straight off me. But tell him I won't cry rape because I like it rough. Let him know I'm looking forward to next time." With a wink and a smirk, the woman turned and sashayed to the elevator.

Tatum stood dumbfounded as the woman stepped inside and gave Tatum a final wave as the doors closed. And that's when Tatum gathered her bearings and ran to the elevator, pounding on the doors like a madwoman.

She waited for what seemed like an eternity for the elevator to return and take her to the lobby. Once downstairs, she ran out the doors of the building, her hazel eyes burning with fury as she looked down each direction of the sidewalk hoping to spot the rude and disrespectful woman who had the gall to come to her home, but she saw no sign of her.

Tatum turned to go back inside of the building, and she spotted the concierge, Dominic, who appeared to just be returning to the front desk.

"Where were you? Do you know some woman managed to come upstairs and knock on my front door?"

Dominic's eyes widened and his features blanched. "I'm so sorry. I stepped away for only a second."

"Only a second is all it would've taken for her to kill me. What if it had been some deranged fan? I'll be talking to King about this," Tatum said, storming back upstairs.

She knew it was wrong to take her frustration out on Dominic. He'd always been so polite to her and King, but Tatum was a ball of emotions, and anyone in her path would bear the brunt of her anger.

Once back inside of the apartment, Tatum picked up a bridal magazine and started tearing out the pages. She picked up another and threw it across the room, letting out a wail of fury and outrage. Picking up her phone, she called King, glad it was still early afternoon and he hadn't taken the court yet for their evening game in Chicago.

"Hey, baby," he answered.

"One of your little tramps just left here."

"What?"

"You heard me. Some woman was just here, and she threw her panties in my face, telling me all about how you ripped them off her the other night and gave her rough sex. You still making a fool of me, King?"

"Tatum, I haven't been with anyone else since we got back together. She's probably some groupie I used to hang out with to pass the time during our breakup, and she's just out for revenge now that we're back together."

"Tell me this then, King: How did she know exactly where to find our apartment? You brought your tramps here once I moved out? Were they in our bed?" Tatum demanded to know.

"Tay, how are we gonna move on if you keep living in the past?"

"Then tell your past not to show up here and throw her dirty drawers in my face."

"Look, I'm gonna talk to building management about this because this crazy chick shouldn't have been able to get access like that."

"King, I already chewed Dominic out, now stop changing the subject."

"Tatum, baby, we're gonna have to talk about this later. I done told you about not getting in my head space with negative energy before I take the court. I have to go. But baby, I love you, and I promise I meant it when I said I want our relationship and upcoming marriage to work."

Once Tatum hung up, some of the anger had diminished, and she wondered if she possibly overreacted, and the woman was indeed someone King had hooked up with once she'd left him. She realized she had no right to be upset with him, but she was still infuriated that she'd allowed the chick to get away with such a disrespectful act.

Tatum called her mother, Vanessa, and filled her in on the entire exchange.

"Let me get this straight: You allowed that hooker to get on the elevator and leave the building after flinging her nasty panties in your face? Tatum, what is wrong with you? Now you know I didn't raise you to put up with any mess like that. You remember when I told you that you needed to lay down the law with these thirsty women out here? Word could soon travel that you're soft, and you'll soon have a bunch of other females trying to test and disrespect you."

"Mama, I didn't call you for a lecture."

"You're right, baby. I'm sorry. Look, like King said, it was probably just some salty female he messed with who's now mad because he's given her walking papers. Don't go making a big deal about this and keep your eyes open at all times. Some of these women out here are crazy, and I'm just glad she had a thong and not a gun."

"Really, Mom? Interesting choice of words. Well, look I know you have to get ready for your shift, so I'll talk to you later."

"I'm counting down the days until you and King tie the knot so I can retire from nursing. Love you, baby."

Tatum sighed at her mother's words, shaking her head. She walked into the bedroom and disrobed so she could shower and head over to Ariana's home where she would watch tonight's game with her and Kelsea. Once she was dressed and had grabbed her purse to leave, she noticed the card with the private investigator's info still inside. She'd never gotten around to tossing it out like she'd planned, and now she figured it was divine intervention that she hadn't. Sighing, she exited the apartment and went downstairs to wait for the car service to take her to Ariana's.

When she arrived, her friends took one look at her face and could tell something was wrong. She filled them in on what transpired earlier that afternoon while sipping on the homemade margarita Ariana had prepared. Ariana listened as she cooked up a delicious smelling Mexican cuisine.

"I still can't believe she threw her panties in my face," Tatum finished. "I must've scrubbed my face and fingers for over an hour in the shower."

"Believe it or not, these groupies have done far worse. Girl, I've been at parties at a player's home where the player had sex with another woman while his wife was downstairs. Then once they were done, the woman came back downstairs and was talking and laughing with the wife like she hadn't just been in the bed with her husband. Yes, honey these groupies are ruthless," Kelsea said.

"That's why I don't trust any females other than you guys. After today, I'm going to be suspicious of any woman trying to be friendly with me. You just never know who the enemy is," Tatum said, gulping down her margarita. She grabbed the pitcher and poured herself another.

"Describe the chick that came to your door," Ariana said.

"She was young and kind of reminded me of Nicki Minaj. She has those slanted eyes, and I can tell she is part Asian."

Ariana whipped out her phone, and after a couple of taps, she showed Tatum an Instagram page.

"That's her," Tatum said. "You know her?"

"No, but I saw King with her a couple of times after you left," Ariana said.

Tatum was shocked to learn the girl was only nineteen, and she was an Instagram model by the name of Ireland.

"Look, have you reached out to the PI yet? I'm telling you; she will inform you about all of the women King has seen or is connected to. This way, you won't be blindsided if one of them ever approaches you again."

"I still have the card. Yes. I'm gonna call this lady first thing tomorrow," Tatum said.

"Man, you should've run and grabbed a knife, or something to bludgeon ole girl with. You could've claimed self-defense and gotten away with it," Ariana joked.

"If King doesn't watch himself, I'm gonna take Wesley up on his offer," Tatum said, then filled them in on Wesley coming on to her at her birthday party.

"Keep his offer in the wings, then give him the goods if you find out King is still stepping out on you. It's the perfect revenge," Ariana encouraged.

"Girl, no. That's the *worst* thing you can do. Never sleep with your man's teammates. All it will serve to do is get you a sordid reputation, and word will fly around the league. You don't want other players coming at you like you're just another groupie chick. Remember, guys are forgiven more for their indiscretions than women," Kelsea schooled, "and if you even look in Antoine's direction, I'm gonna give you the beat down you should've given Ireland."

They all shared a laugh and prepared to dig into Ariana's homemade enchiladas, tamales, refried beans, and Spanish rice. Being with her friends helped cheer Tatum up and take her mind off the afternoon's drama. She hated the idea of returning home to an empty apartment. She couldn't wait for King's flight to arrive so they could talk and try to resolve this latest dilemma.

***

"I promise you, Tatum, I've never slept with Ireland. We only went out to dinner a few times, and I discovered she was immature and childish. To be honest, she's been stalking me since we've gotten back together, and I've seriously considered getting a restraining order against her. She's even traveled to the same cities where I have games. I'm telling you, she's crazy. She managed to find out where I live and sneak past security. That's exactly why I've had Dominic fired. Tatum, I wouldn't be able to live with myself if she'd harmed you." King had been pouring his heart out to Tatum since he'd arrived home.

"Why didn't you tell me about this before, especially if you felt she was dangerous?"

"Because I was scared you wouldn't believe me and leave again," King said.

Tatum felt her heart softening. He pulled her to him, and they shared a kiss before falling upon the bed and showing just how much they loved each other.

Hours later, while still entwined in King's arms, Tatum was awakened by a text alert from her phone. Disengaging herself from her slumbering fiancé, Tatum grabbed her phone from the nightstand and saw Kelsea had sent her a link to The Jasmine Brand Instagram page that featured an interview from an anonymous source detailing how King Watts' fiancée had been confronted at their luxury apartment by his sidepiece. Tatum figured the 'source' was Dominic. All building employees had to sign a non-disclosure agreement, so this was his sly and underhanded way of retaliating against Tatum and King for getting him fired.

Tatum's phone rang, and Gya's name flashed on the screen. Thinking her cousin was calling about the article, she went into the living room so as not to awaken King, whom she was certain would be livid once he learned that Dominic had gone to the tabloids.

"Tatum, what's going on? Who is this girl Ireland? She did an IG live talking about having sex with King."

Tatum's eyes nearly bulged out of her head. "What?"

"I've had several followers tag me on her IG page. She's saved the livestream and I watched a bit of it before having to turn it off in disgust. She goes into pretty graphic detail."

"She's a crazy psychopath who is nothing but a liar. Let me call you back," Tatum said.

Tatum went to Ireland's page and felt her stomach churning as she watched the immature twit describe how King slid into her DMs and flirted with her before they exchanged numbers. She thought she would vomit when Ireland spoke about King's stellar bedroom skills, citing that he gave new meaning to the term *hung like a horse*. The comment section went crazy when Ireland detailed how she'd thrown her thong in Tatum's face. Tatum grew dizzy at the fast pace of the comments and the various types of emojis egging Ireland on. Having seen and heard enough, Tatum clicked off the video, filled with disgust. She stormed into the bedroom, flipping on the light, and picking up a pillow to throw at King. It hit him square in the center of his forehead.

"*Ouch*. Tatum, what the hell?" King sat up, his eyes darting around wildly in confusion, trying to adjust to the sudden brightness of the bedroom.

"You lied to me again, King. Your little whore was on IG live telling the world about how good you are in bed. Why do you insist on making a fool of me?"

"What? We're really doing this again? Tatum, for the last time, she is lying."

"Dominic has been talking to gossip blogs. One of them posted a story about Ireland showing up at our apartment. That story is probably why she decided to go live on IG and bask in her little fifteen minutes of fame."

"Man, forget that chump, Dominic. And Ireland too. Why are you waking me up out of my sleep with this nonsense? You know it's not often I get to be at home and rest."

"You know what, keep on, King. I'm gonna take Wesley up on his offer if you keep trying me."

Tatum turned to leave the room, but King shot up like a rocket and was across the room in an instant, grabbing her by her arm.

"What did you just say? You're gonna do what? Did Wesley try to step to you?"

"Boy, let go of my arm. Are you crazy, putting your hands on me?"

"No, tell me now," King said, grabbing her by both arms and shaking her.

Tatum wrestled out of his grasp. "Don't you ever put your hands on me again."

King brought his index finger to the tip of her nose. "If you even think about messing around with Wesley, I promise you, Tatum, I'll kill you both."

"You're seriously threatening me? Oh, you big mad, huh? You can dish your dirt but can't take it. You've cheated on me, but the mere thought of me messing around on you sends you into a rage? You've got some nerve."

"I mean it, Tatum, if you value your life, don't think about trying me." King glared at her and went back into their bedroom, slamming the door.

Minutes later, Tatum heard the shower running.

Tatum considered calling the police and reporting King for assault, but she didn't want to fuel the flames of the latest controversy they found themselves embroiled in. Would she ever be able to catch a break?

Chapter Twenty-one

Tatum and King slept in separate rooms, and once she heard him leave for practice the next morning, she got up and got herself together. She was in the middle of cooking breakfast when Gya phoned.

"I was just calling to check on you. I can relate to what you're going through since this Ireland girl is just as young as Mercedes. I'm in prayer about this entire situation, cousin."

"How is Bryant recuperating?"

"His knee seems to be healing fine, but he's still down in the dumps about not being able to play. We're still seeing a therapist once a week, and the sessions are working, as we're re-establishing our bond. I feel there's hope for us."

Tatum was happy for her cousin, but she wished she could say the same. She'd spoken with Vanessa earlier, and she'd been on a rampage about Ireland's video, fretting that more women would be coming at King now to see if his bedroom prowess was as stellar as Ireland described. She also reiterated that women would try testing her since Ireland boasted about the thong-throwing stunt.

After hanging up with Gya, Tatum was in the middle of eating breakfast when Kelsea phoned.

"Are you watching ESPN? King and Wesley got into another scuffle during practice."

Tatum's heart dropped.

"I just talked to Antoine, and he told me they were fighting because King confronted him about you. Now Tatum, are you sure you haven't slept with Wesley? Did King find out about it?"

"Kelsea, I can't believe you're asking me this. I'm not messing with Wesley in any form or fashion, but I did threaten King that I would if he kept stepping out on me. Of course, I didn't mean it."

"The rumor mill is already churning that you slept with Wesley to get back at King about this Ireland business."

Tatum placed a hand to her throbbing temple, feeling a migraine coming on. "Kelsea, let me call you back. I need a glass of wine."

***

It was a week before Christmas, and Tatum was waiting within the tunnel of the arena after the Flash game. The team was on a losing streak, and King and Wesley had been fined by the team owner for their fight in practice. Things were still tense between Tatum and King since the Ireland incident. His road games didn't leave a lot of time for them to talk, which was just as well for Tatum. She was once again in a state of confusion concerning their relationship and needed the space.

Now as she waited for him to come out of the locker room, she was going to suggest they have a late evening dinner, her way of extending an olive branch toward re-opening the lines of communication between them. She didn't want to spend Christmas at odds. It was her favorite holiday, and it had already gotten off to a gloomy start. She hadn't been in the holiday spirit since.

A beautiful blond, white woman approached her with a smile. "Hello, Tatum."

Tatum was instantly guarded. "Do I know you?"

"No. I'm just waiting for King," the blond replied.

"Oh really?" Tatum slapped the woman across the face. "Don't you ever disrespect me and tell me you're waiting for my man. You understand?"

The woman grabbed her cheek and looked at Tatum in horror.

A crowd formed as Tatum lunged at the woman, and a couple of players had come to restrain her.

"You stay the hell away from my fiancé," Tatum shouted.

***

The following morning in Miami, Gya awakened to the news that Tatum had been arrested for physically assaulting a female sports reporter.

Gya immediately phoned her cousin. When Tatum answered, she sounded as if she had been crying.

"Gya, I can't believe I lost it like that. I thought the woman was trying to taunt me about King. I had no idea she was a reporter."

Tatum explained that King had come to the police station and posted her bail. Her court date was set for after the holidays.

"Let's just pray for favor that this woman will drop the charges. I mean, if I were you, I would try to contact her and explain the misunderstanding. Hopefully, as a fellow woman, she'll be sympathetic."

"I doubt it, and I honestly wouldn't blame her if she goes forward with pressing charges. I deserve it." Tatum broke down in tears, and it twisted at Gya's heart to hear her favorite cousin in such a state of distress. She immediately went into prayer right there on the phone, asking God to show grace and mercy upon Tatum.

After hanging up, Gya saw that social media was going crazy discussing the incident. Sports critics mentioned the Flash's recent losing streak and blamed the losses on King's off-court distractions. Gya was disgusted by some of the distasteful jokes and innuendo. People were speculating that King was messing around with the reporter, and rumors were circulating that he and Tatum had engaged in a threesome. Another rumor circulating was that the reporter had asked Tatum if she was sleeping with Wesley Johnson, which was why Tatum had slapped her. Even Gya and Bryant had gotten dragged into the controversy with people joking that Tatum slapped the reporter for asking if the Waves were making the playoffs and Gya should've taught her cousin more Christ-like attributes. By that evening, Tatum had been smeared and labeled as a typical angry black woman with some race-baiting pundits writing think pieces citing that it would be poetic justice for King to leave Tatum and start dating the reporter. One even went so far as to write that her behavior was the reason black men chose to date outside of their race. Gya was infuriated. Social media never ceased to amaze her with its nastiness, cruelty, and misjudgments.

Having seen and read enough, Gya just logged off altogether and prayed God would see her cousin through the eye of this latest storm.

Chapter Twenty-two

"You know, Tatum, my father always says, 'Where there's smoke, there's fire.' I can't turn a blind eye to all this talk about you and Wesley. Look me in my eyes right now and tell me there is nothing going on between the two of you," King demanded.

Tatum was about to head into the bathroom to take a nice long bath, hoping the water and soapy suds would help alleviate the tension in her muscles, but she whirled around and glared at her fiancé. "Are you serious right now, King?"

"Tatum, I'm gonna be honest: All this craziness with you assaulting that reporter has embarrassed the hell out of me. How could you behave like that? You know I have to maintain a certain image, and now my fiancée is slapping people, acting like a common hoodrat."

"Let's talk about what led me to slap her to begin with, shall we? Given your past indiscretions, please excuse me for being mistrustful of these females out here."

King sighed. "Look, don't try and deflect. We're past all that Ireland and STD mess. Don't use that as an excuse for your insecurities and paranoia."

"No, you're the one who's being paranoid and deflecting. You know good and well I'm not messing around with Wesley."

"I don't know anything," King shot back. "My teammates are laughing behind my back about it, and Wesley is always smirking when he sees me, as if he knows something I don't."

"Nothing is going on with me and Wesley. He just enjoys trying to get in your head. Now don't ask me that foolishness again."

***

Later while King was at a team practice, Kelsea and Ariana came over to the apartment for lunch. They wanted to go out to a restaurant, but Tatum didn't want to be seen out in public just yet, fearing she'd be hounded by paparazzi and gossip blog reporters. They ordered in food and lounged around in the living room, the wintry backdrop of Manhattan on full display through the massive windows of the apartment.

"Well, Tatum, at least you don't have to worry about any female trying you again," Kelsea joked.

"You sound like my mom," Tatum said wryly with a roll of her eyes.

"And just what did Mama Vanessa have to say about all this?" Ariana asked, taking a bite of her salmon tartare salad.

"Her main concern is making sure my engagement to King is still intact and not affected," Tatum said with frustration. "The wedding planning is all she ever wants to talk about now. She sees this assault incident as nothing but a distraction. I just wish she'd be more supportive of my emotions and feelings. All she's concerned about is King."

"I mean, I can't fault her for wanting the best for her daughter," Kelsea said.

"The 'best' would be a man who didn't cheat on me," Tatum said, taking a sip of wine.

"I do agree that this is just a distraction. You lost your head for a minute. It happens to the best of us. I'm sure King will settle with this reporter, and she'll drop the charges. It'll all blow over soon. By next week, the media will be focused on something else," Ariana assured.

And she was right. The following week, King informed Tatum he'd reached a settlement with the woman, and she would drop all charges on the condition of a public apology from Tatum. Tatum obliged and posted the apology to social media, and she called the reporter to apologize personally as well.

Jacoby was in town, and he and King were preparing to go to dinner. Jacoby accosted Tatum while she was in the kitchen fixing an evening snack as King was showering.

"I hope you realize paying off this reporter wasn't cheap, Tatum. I hope you'll keep a low profile from now on and not do anything to put my son in these types of situations in the future."

"We're good over here, Jacoby. But I'm curious: Do you plan to give this same pep talk to King—telling him to keep his junk in his pants and not have IG sluts coming to our front door?"

Tatum couldn't believe how boldly she was talking to King's father, but she didn't appreciate him coming into their home trying to check her.

Jacoby chuckled. "Men will be men, Tatum. You're not that naïve as to where you didn't know what you were signing up for from the minute you first began dating King."

Tatum looked thoughtful. "Men will be men," she repeated. "It's interesting you would say that. Were you just being a man when you stepped out on Mrs. Michelle and produced your outside child?"

Tatum had to keep from smirking in satisfaction as she heard Jacoby's sharp intake of breath.

"Tell me, Jacoby, is King aware that a portion of the money you're taking as his business manager is going toward child support? Nah, of course he isn't."

Jacoby laughed and attempted to wave her off. "Tatum, you really are crazy. Perhaps I need to have a talk with King about calling off this engagement. You're clearly unhinged."

"You do that, Jacoby, and I'll have no choice but to tell King all about his eight-year-old brother. And that on top of paying child support, you're also paying this child's mother hush money. Can't have her trying to cash in on King's newfound fame and tell the world all about his half-brother. If you continue to interfere in me and King's relationship, I'll be the one to tell the world about your lowdown cheating ways. Such a pity because I know your secrets would destroy Mrs. Michelle, and I'm sure King would kick your behind to the curb if he found out about your double life," Tatum threatened, her eyes blazing with malice.

She watched as Jacoby swallowed hard and glared at her. He had no idea that she'd hired the PI to not only trail King but to get dirt on Jacoby as well to use as leverage. He initially tried to call her bluff, but the accuracy of the child's gender and age had him rendered into silence.

"Now if you don't want your precious secrets being revealed, I strongly suggest that you talk to King about being faithful and marrying me without a prenup. Also, ensure the wedding takes place by our intended date. I don't want to hear any excuses from King about waiting or pushing back the date," Tatum demanded.

"I can't believe I was so wrong about you, Tatum. I thought you were the sweetest person when King first brought you home, and now you're standing here threatening to tear my family apart. Threatening to turn my son against me? You know King thinks the world of me," Jacoby finally spoke.

"King thinks the world of a fraud. I'd be doing him a favor by pulling the blinders off his eyes and exposing you for the lying and deceitful scum of a man and father you are,"

With a final glare, Jacoby stormed out of the kitchen. Tatum exhaled, leaning against the counter. Who was this woman she was turning into? She'd literally just blackmailed her fiancé's father. But Tatum was tired of being pushed around by them both.

The PI revealed that King was still creeping around with Ireland. While Tatum still truly loved King, she now viewed their upcoming nuptials as a business arrangement. If King was intent on stepping out with other women, then Tatum wanted to be compensated for any pain and humiliation, hence removing the notion of signing any form of prenuptial agreement. After today's conversation, she had no doubt that Jacoby would convince King to drop the idea.

I'm just securing my future like my mother advised, Tatum thought while sipping another glass of red wine.

Chapter Twenty-three

The Flash had an away game Christmas evening. Vanessa flew in on Christmas Eve to spend the holiday with Tatum. She was still sleeping in the guest room when Tatum awakened on Christmas morning. Tatum's festive spirit was dampened by the fact that she was spending her favorite holiday without her man. She walked into the living room to see snow falling, and she looked over at the frosted white Christmas tree Ariana and Kelsea had helped her erect and decorate with gold shimmering ornaments.

Tatum contemplated if she should open the gifts King had left underneath the tree now or wait until he returned home. But her anxiousness wouldn't allow her to wait any longer. She tore into each gift. She received glistening jewelry from Tiffany's, designer purses, and clothing. But the one thing she wanted couldn't be wrapped, and that was King's devotion and fidelity.

Tatum turned on Sirius XM's Holiday Soul channel and went into the kitchen to eat a bagel with cream cheese accompanied by a cup of coffee. Whitney Houston's "Who Would Imagine a King" began to play. It had always been one of Tatum's favorite Christmas songs. Tatum sat in the kitchen eating and listening to the song in a contemplative state of silence when Vanessa walked inside, her eyes glowing with excitement as she took in Tatum's gifts.

"Ooh, I can't wait to see what King got me," Vanessa said in lieu of a good morning or a Merry Christmas.

"Knock yourself out, Mom," Tatum said, standing and preparing to wash her empty plate and cup.

"No breakfast for your mother?"

"All I had was a bagel. You want that?" Tatum asked dryly.

"Girl, what is wrong with you? Where is your Christmas spirit?" Vanessa asked, frowning.

Tatum sighed. She wished her mother would just leave because she wasn't in a jovial mood. She was bitter about having to share her man with the NBA on this special holiday. Tatum spent the better part of the day watching *A Christmas Story* on TNT. The Flash versus the Lakers game followed, and Tatum tuned in, hoping the Flash could secure a Christmas victory.

***

Gya had a very Merry Christmas with Bryant and her family in Houston. The following day, she was inspired to write a book. It would be titled *Well Worth the Wait,* and she made a decision to be very candid about all of the controversies she'd faced since becoming an NFL wife, including Bryant's adultery. The book would serve as a devotional and prayer journal. She worked on it nonstop over the next two weeks.

She and Bryant attended Watch Night Service at church. Gya wanted to embark upon the new year with a spiritual renewal to God as well as to her marriage. She even felt confident about trying to conceive another baby.

***

Gya wasn't the only one trying to establish a fresh start for the new year. King called a truce with Tatum, wanting to enter January with a clean slate from all the craziness of the past year. They spent New Year's Eve dining at the restaurant, Eleven Madison Park. Tatum was candid with King, revealing she knew he was still seeing Ireland and that a part of her knew Ireland was telling the truth when she confronted her that afternoon at their apartment.

"Can I be honest, Tatum, without you thinking I'm being corny?"

Tatum merely raised an eyebrow, and King took that as his cue to continue. "Being with Ireland, it fed my ego. In the beginning, I wasn't getting as much playing time with the Flash as I was used to. Ireland is nineteen and being with her reminded me of my early college days at UCLA—being the star on campus. I missed that. That's all my dealings with her symbolized. I'm not in love with her by any means. She just filled a void."

"King, save me the sob stories and excuses, okay?"

King sucked his teeth. "See, you women wonder why dudes can't be upfront and vulnerable with y'all."

"So, tell me this, do you regret entering the NBA early? Do you wish you'd finished college?"

"Yes. Sometimes I wonder if I made a mistake. Perhaps I wasn't mature enough or ready for all this lifestyle entailed."

Tatum nodded in understanding.

116

"Look, my dad had a nice, long talk with me. He told me it's time to buckle down and grow up. Starting with becoming your husband."

Tatum had to suppress a smirk. *I'll just bet he did,* she thought.

King grabbed Tatum's hands from across the table, bringing the hand adorning his engagement ring to his lips and kissing it. "I want to start doing right by you, Tatum. I'm human, and I can't promise I'll never disappoint you or let you down again, but, baby, right here and now, I'm vowing to do my very best. Daily."

Tatum had to keep from rolling her eyes because she knew King was doing nothing but making empty promises once again.

King lifted his glass for a toast. "Here's to new beginnings."

Tatum acquiesced, lifting her own glass to clink against his. "I'm going to hold you to your word, King."

King nodded and sipped, failing to notice Tatum's eyes cut and narrow at him over the rim of her champagne glass.

Chapter Twenty-four

Gya's book was completed within three weeks and then sent off to an editor. She'd begun marketing and promotion at the beginning of the new year so her legions of followers were greatly anticipating the release of the book, which she would self-publish. The book was scheduled to be released in mid-March.

Valentine's Day weekend marked the NBA All-Star festivities, which was being held in Miami that year. But since Bryant and Gya were spending Valentine's Day in the Maldives, Tatum wouldn't get an opportunity to see Gya while she was in town.

Tatum had to admit that King seemed to be honoring the pledge he'd made to her on New Year's Eve. He called her every night whenever he was on the road for away games. It was to the point where Tatum was comfortable with relieving the PI of her duties, given that King seemed to be much more attentive and loving. Friday night of All Star weekend found her at the FTX arena cheering King on from the stands as he participated in the Rising Stars Challenge, a game in which rookies played against sophomore players. Tatum beamed as King racked up several points and was crowned as game MVP.

Winning MVP set King ablaze as he went on to win the slam dunk competition the following evening.

During Sunday's All-Star game, the national anthem was sung by the sultry R&B singer Gemini, a talented songstress who hailed from Houston and was married to the rapper turned businessman Dakari "Iced Thug" Redding. The music industry's power couple were the parents of two beautiful girls. Tatum recalled the controversial shooting of Gemini years ago and was glad to see the singer fully recovered and thriving.

As she sat taking in the All-Star game with Kelsea and Ariana, they filled her in on all the latest NBA gossip and happenings.

"You know Jarad Rolands plays for Atlanta now that's he's been traded from the Houston Asteroids. I heard he pushed for the trade so he could be closer to the daughter he has with his ex-wife Melodie, but Melodie is now married to an Atlanta Falcon. Talk about awkward, right?" Kelsea laughed.

"How old is the son he had with that college groupie? What was her name? Skyye, I think," Ariana asked.

"Yeah. He should be about four years old now since both Melodie and Skyye were pregnant at the same time. Jarad was a real piece of work. Anyway, she's opened a soul food restaurant in Dallas called The Skyye is the Limit. I'm sure she's used the child support money to fund her business, but hey, I ain't mad," Kelsea said, taking a sip of her cocktail.

The East ended up beating the West team, and following the game, King was approached by reps from Pepsi. They wanted to set up a future meeting to discuss an endorsement deal, which would include a commercial featuring footage from King's stellar performance in the slam-dunk contest.

When King and Tatum returned to their apartment the following Monday, a trail of rose petals greeted them. Tatum turned to King, her eyes questioning. For a split second, she wondered if some groupie had gained access to their apartment, but when she saw the Cheshire cat grin on King's handsome features, she knew her man had planned this romantic surprise. He led her by the hand to a table set for two with cuisine from Carbone's, which had become her favorite Italian restaurant in New York City. Tatum's mouth watered as she took in the lobster ravioli, Caesar salad, garlic bread, and Pinot Noir along with a slice of decadent strawberry cheesecake.

"I cleared it with building management to allow the decorators and the restaurant caterers to have access to our apartment and set up before we arrived."

"So, is this why you wanted to wait until this morning to leave Miami? I was ready to fly back home last night after the game."

King kissed her full, luscious lips. "Yep. Didn't want to ruin my surprise."

They dined and then retreated to their warmed and bubbling Jacuzzi-style tub, after which they spent the remainder of the evening within the throes of passion, falling asleep wrapped in each other's arms.

The next morning, a masseuse came to the apartment to give them both massages.

"King, I'm speechless," Tatum said.

"Since we had to sacrifice our Valentine's Day weekend for All-Star, I wanted to make it up to you. I plan to lavish and love on you all week long, baby," King said with a sexy wink.

After the massages, they ventured out to have lunch at Shuko's where they discussed more wedding planning details.

"I want us to start on a family as soon as we're married, Tatum. Honestly, I want to be a girl dad like Kobe Bryant."

Tatum's eyes widened. "Seriously? I just knew you'd want a couple of boys."

King shook his head. "Nah. I don't want my son feeling pressured to play basketball or live up to my image. I've heard LeBron James discuss this happening to his sons."

Tatum nodded in understanding. "Well of course we can't control gender. Whatever God allows me to have, I'll be okay with. Besides, our son could wind up just as gifted athletically as you. Shoot, he may surpass you." Tatum laughed.

King looked solemn. "There's another reason I don't want a boy. Suppose he ends up gay like Korey?"

Tatum frowned. "What if he does? Even though I don't agree with that lifestyle, I'd love him just the same."

King sucked his teeth. "I refuse to have a gay son tarnishing my name. If we do have a son, don't name him after me, just in case."

Tatum's eyes ballooned. "King, do you hear how ignorant you sound right now?"

"I'm serious. Besides, LeBron said he regrets naming his son after him, due to the expectations people tend to place on a junior. I feel the same way, either way. I don't want my son named after me."

"And if it's a girl and she turns out to be a lesbian, then what?"

King shrugged. "For some reason that wouldn't bother me as much as having a gay son."

"Need I remind you that Magic Johnson and Dwyane Wade fully support their gay sons?"

"Look, good for them. Let's change the subject 'cause I can sense you're getting an attitude, and I don't want to ruin what's supposed to be a romantic week over an argument about kids that aren't even born yet."

Tatum agreed because she was so close to going off on King for being so bigoted. He was more like Jacoby than she realized.

***

During the off-season, Bryant was working out religiously to fully rehab his knee and get in shape for his sophomore season after such a disappointing rookie year. Bryant couldn't even bear to watch the Super Bowl, hating that the Waves missed their shot at winning the Lombardi trophy. Bryant direly wanted to go to the championship game and would do everything possible next season to make it happen. He was also adamant about reconnecting with God after his fall from grace due to his act of infidelity.

Gya experienced bouts of nausea during their trip to the Maldives. Once arriving back to Miami, a positive pregnancy test confirmed her suspicions: She and Bryant were expecting again. Bryant had concerns about her plans to still go on the promo tour her publicist had scheduled to start in March once her book was released, but she assured him her OB/GYN stated that traveling would be fine.

"So, it looks like we can still visit St. Barts once the tour has concluded in June," Gya said, sealing their plans with a kiss.

Finally, her home life was back on track, and she was excited about their future family now that all the craziness was behind them.

Chapter Twenty-five

Although the Flash gained momentum after the All-Star break, the wins weren't enough to secure a playoff spot. King decided to jumpstart his off season by attending the Final Four championship games in Ohio at the beginning of April. Unfortunately, UCLA had a lackluster season after King's departure, and many die-hard fans faulted him for the sinking ship of a team he left in his wake. The Bruins didn't even qualify for the March Madness games. Some sports critics and fans called King selfish for not finishing his senior year and giving the Bruins a shot at a repeat championship title. Others argued that the performance of a team shouldn't lie upon the shoulders of one player. Nevertheless, King was welcomed and embraced once gracing the University of Dayton arena with his presence. King's overall popularity skyrocketed with NBA fans after winning the All-Star Slam Dunk competition. He'd become a lucrative commodity overnight with several brands and products seeking to secure endorsement deals with an emerging NBA superstar.

Tatum stayed behind in New York City, battling what she assumed was a flu bug, but her OB/GYN told her something different.

"Pregnant?" Tatum repeated, her hazel eyes ballooning.

"Yes, ma'am," Dr. Rosario confirmed. "You're about eight weeks along."

Tatum did the calculations and determined she conceived during the surprise romantic rendezvous week King planned after All-Star weekend.

"Dr. Rosario, how is this possible when I'm on birth control?"

"Do you take it consistently?" Dr. Rosario asked.

"Yes. I mean there have been a couple of times I've missed a dose. After drinking a bit of wine, I got drowsy and went to sleep, but I'd take it first thing the next morning."

"Of course, you can consume alcohol while taking the pill, but missing dosages can decrease its effectiveness."

Tatum's heart was pounding. A baby? She was going to be a mother by Christmas? Granted, she and King were engaged and had plans to start a family, but this took her by total surprise.

Dr. Rosario instructed her to begin prenatal vitamins and wanted her to come in for regular checkups to monitor her closely throughout the first trimester.

Tatum left the office in a daze. She had a feeling King, as well as her mother, would be happy about the news. Gya may turn her nose up at the thought of Tatum being pregnant out of wedlock. But the thought of walking down the aisle in a few months with a swollen belly didn't sit well with Tatum either. She didn't want to look like a bloated whale in her wedding photos.

Tatum shared the news with King as soon as he returned from the championship game where the Baylor Bears had won the title. Tatum noticed he seemed a bit on edge, jittery, and distracted. She wondered if all the negative talk concerning the fate of the Bruins had gotten under his skin, yet King surprised her by blurting out, "Let's elope."

Tatum blinked. "Elope?"

"Yes. Let's go to Vegas tonight and do it."

Tatum laughed. "King, are you serious?"

"Yes, baby. Let's do this."

"But King, I really wanted a big wedding. I mean, we only have three more months," Tatum said, referencing their plans to wed during the Fourth of July holiday weekend.

King sighed in exasperation. "Tatum, you were pressing me to propose and hounding me about securing a wedding date, and now that I want to seal the deal, you're hesitating? It's like you're never satisfied."

"It's not like that, King. I mean we've already put so much money into this wedding—"

"We can still have the official ceremony with all of our family and friends in July."

"Why are you so insistent on getting married now? This wouldn't have anything to do with your pending endorsement deals, would it?"

"To be honest, yes. My father wants to be sure I don't do anything to taint my image, and honestly, being a baby daddy is not a good look."

"So why not just announce the pregnancy after our wedding?"

"Tatum, seriously? You'll be showing soon. C'mon, baby. Stop fighting me on this. I want to make you my wife *tonight*."

Tatum sighed and nodded. "Okay, King."

She called her mother to inform her of their plans to elope and about the pregnancy. Vanessa was ecstatic and planned to meet them in Vegas, wanting to be present for the nuptials. Tatum called Gya as well, and her cousin congratulated her on the news. Unfortunately, she couldn't fly into Vegas due to being in Houston for a book tour appearance, and she also had a women's ministry speaking engagement scheduled with her childhood church.

"I can't believe the both of us are pregnant at the same time. Our children are going to be so close," Gya gushed.

True to his words, King whisked Tatum off on a private chartered jet to Las Vegas, and they wed at The Venetian hotel in the presence of Vanessa, Michelle, Jacoby, and even King's brother, Korey.

Since she was not yet showing, Tatum donned the strapless mermaid style dress she'd selected for their wedding in July. After sealing their union with a long, sultry kiss, the two headed off for an impromptu honeymoon in Florence, Italy.

***

Gya had been on a high since the start of her book tour, and her hometown of Houston had been a magnificent stop on her schedule. She basked in the love and warmth she received from the women during her book signing, as well as the women's ministry event at her home church. She was fully walking in her purpose and cherishing every moment of it. It was her prayer that her book would bless many women, and God was showing His faithfulness, not just with the success of her book and ministry, but also with giving her another chance at motherhood. She'd proudly announced her pregnancy to the public at the start of her tour.

A week after her Houston stop, Gya was back in Miami doing a signing at a local bookstore when a woman approached her table. A lady next to her appeared to be filming from her camera phone.

"Congratulations on the newest addition to your family," the woman said with a syrupy sweet smile.

"Thank you for your kind words and well wishes," Gya said, returning the woman's smile.

"Gya, we're live on IG and inquiring minds want to know if you'll accept the daughter Bryant has with another woman and allow her to be raised alongside the child you're expecting?" the woman asked, with the smile still plastered across her face.

Gya blinked, her smile quickly replaced with a frown. "I beg your pardon?"

The woman held up her cell phone, which had a photo of Bryant in what looked like a hospital room, holding a newborn baby.

"This is Bryant's first child," she said, holding the phone up to Gya and then turning to display the photo to the camera her friend was holding. "So again I ask, will you accept his newborn daughter or shun her?" the woman pressed.

Gya's publicist, Amy, intervened. "Ma'am, this is not the place for this. You both need to leave. Stop that livestream immediately." She gestured for security, and they escorted the women away.

The woman who had shown the photo tossed a sly smirk and wave over her shoulder at Gya.

Gya's hand shook as she continued to sign books after the exchange. She couldn't believe the maliciousness of some women. It saddened her that someone could be so catty, but she wondered about the photo. Whose child was Bryant holding? She had no doubt it was him in the picture, but could it have been photoshopped? Or perhaps he was pictured with the child of some fan. Bryant was always performing some random act of kindness. Maybe a fan's wish was for Bryant to be pictured cradling his newborn.

The book signing wrapped up soon after, to Gya's utter relief, because the prior exchange with the petty woman had left her nerves rattled. Once she and Amy were in their chauffeured black Tahoe SUV, Amy dropped a bombshell.

"I did a bit of digging, Gya, and it seems that a girl named Mercedes Diaz gave birth to a baby daughter about two weeks ago. Allegedly, Bryant is the father."

Gya's heart plummeted into her chest. Mercedes Diaz was Christal's cousin. But how was that possible? Bryant assured her Mercedes was lying about being pregnant.

"I put a call in to one of my contacts at TMZ, and they're about to break the story. Turns out Bryant paid Mercedes some hush money to recant her story about being pregnant. There was a private settlement reached in terms of prenatal care and child support, but somehow news of the birth has leaked."

Gya felt like she was in a black tunnel, and Amy's words were distant, like a mere drone in her ear. Once again, her heart felt like it was being ripped out of her chest. Could this be true? Had Bryant covered up Mercedes's pregnancy? How could the man she was just learning to trust again keep up this charade and lie to her for all these months? When had Bryant become so duplicitous?

Once Gya walked into the home they shared and took one look at Bryant's guilty eyes, they told everything she needed to know—everything she was hoping wasn't true and was just a misunderstanding. She wanted it all to be a lie, but the only thing that seemed to be a lie was the illusion of her happy and thriving marriage.

Gya and Bryant seemed to be in state of suspended animation as they stood and stared at each other. Gya realized that Christal was aware of the ruse and probably inwardly laughed at Gya whenever their paths crossed at Waves games. Yes, she was sure Christal, Mercedes, and all of the Waves WAGs had a good laugh at her expense. She realized her entire ministry and brand was a complete and utter joke.

"I just saw the story on TMZ. Baby...I'm so sorry. Please.... let me explain," Bryant stuttered.

Suddenly, the house was filled with an almost animalistic roar. The sound emerged from the deepest parts of Gya's being. She grabbed a nearby lamp and anything else she could get her hands on, flinging them at Bryant who tried to take cover as Gya went to grab one of his old crutches.

"I'm going to give you a concussion and bust out both of your knees so you'll never be able to play ball again," Gya screamed as she lunged toward him.

Suddenly she felt a check in her spirit, as if the Holy Spirit was giving her pause. Gya lowered her arm, tossed the crutch on the ground, and collapsed into a heap of tears. Deep, guttural sobs emerged from her throat.

Bryant stood crying pitifully as well.

"I'm filing for divorce," Gya said so softly that Bryant wasn't sure he heard her correctly. "I want you out of this house. Get out."

Bryant brooked no argument. He slowly backed away and went upstairs to pack his things.

Gya lost track of all sense of time once he left. All she remembered was going upstairs and lying across their bed still fully clothed and crying herself to sleep.

She was awakened by the ringing of her cell phone and discovered it was well into the next morning. It was her mother telling her that gossip blogs were ablaze with stories about Bryant's illegitimate daughter. Gya's heart broke all over again as she told her mom that the stories were true, and she'd asked Bryant to leave the house.

"I'm catching the next flight out. Please try not to stress about this, Gya, though I know it's easier said than done. I don't want you miscarrying again. This is yet another storm God will get you through. I love you so much, baby girl. I promise Mama is here for you."

After hanging up, Gya pondered her mother's words. And just why was God allowing this to happen? Wasn't she obedient by writing the book and continuing to minister to women? Why was He taking her through such heartache? Why had Bryant seemed to transform before her very eyes? She never thought she'd ever question God, but she didn't understand. She was now angry at the God who she'd thought of as being so faithful and having these types of thoughts scared her. Not only didn't she recognize the person Bryant had become, but she was also slowly losing sight of herself and her faith. How could she continue to lead and guide women toward Christ when her own life was a continual mess of unending heartache and drama?

***

King instituted a no-cell-phone-usage policy while on their honeymoon, and Tatum agreed. He'd given their family and friends instructions to only reach out to them in the event of an emergency, wanting to be caring and attentive toward his new bride. They had a wonderful weeklong honeymoon touring the Tuscany town of Florence. Tatum was wistful as they boarded their return flight home to the States.

After landing at JFK airport and retrieving their luggage from baggage claim, Tatum and King were walking toward their ordered car service vehicle when they were bum-rushed and nearly blinded by the flashing lights of cameras and paparazzi. Tatum anticipated that news of their surprise nuptials would take the media by surprise, but she had no idea it would illicit such an ambush.

The paparazzi cleared a path as a New York City policeman and two white men dressed in white collared shirts, khaki pants, and ties approached King. One of the men flashed a badge.

"Kingsley Watts, I regret to inform you that you're being placed under arrest for rape. Please come with us."

Tatum's mouth dropped open, and she looked at King for an explanation. Was this some type of joke? Were they being featured on a re-launch of that television show *Punk'd*? Tatum's gaze swept around crazily, looking for Ashton Kutcher to make an appearance.

King met Tatum's eyes helplessly. "I'm sorry," he mouthed as the detectives ushered him away amid the continual flashes of camera lights and a barrage of questions from reporters.

***

Now safely back in the confines of their New York City apartment, Tatum escorted the attorney King had hired to the door. The attorney was en route to Dayton, Ohio where King had been transported by authorities and was being held on a half-million-dollar bail. But first he'd filled Tatum in on all the details of the rape allegation King was facing and the impending investigation. Once he left, Tatum grabbed her phone, playing Tamar Braxton's "Crazy Kind of Love" because at that moment, she felt like the biggest dummy of them all. King had played her well, and the entire elopement was nothing more than a ploy to get ahead of the scandal he knew was brewing.

Tatum yearned for a glass of wine but didn't want to consume any alcohol now that she was expecting. Her heart sank as she thought about the baby she was carrying. She was set to give birth to the baby of an alleged rapist.

From what the attorney shared, King had sexual relations with a Baylor college cheerleader after the championship game in Dayton. The following morning, the cheerleader went to the police to report that King raped her. King was discreetly taken to the Dayton police headquarters for questioning. King and his attorney arranged to keep the incident out of the media, and King was allowed to return to New York City. Tatum now realized this was why he seemed so mentally preoccupied when she informed him of her pregnancy. She figured he rushed the wedding so he could paint a family-man image ahead of the rape debacle he knew would emerge.

The media was reporting that King fled the country to escape arrest, but his lawyer insisted King was not given any orders that forbid him to leave the United States. Tatum was so confused. King apparently admitted to investigators that he'd slept with the cheerleader, but according to him, it was consensual. She didn't want to believe King was capable of sexual assault but given his change of attitude since entering the NBA, she felt he was capable of anything. It pained her to have those thoughts about the man she loved; the man who was now her husband and the father of her unborn child. Tatum felt bamboozled. She felt as if King trapped her into marriage so she couldn't easily leave him once the news of the rape allegation broke.

"Well played, King. Well played," Tatum muttered under her breath as she rubbed her belly while looking out into the darkness of the New York City landscape from their apartment window, "but the game is just beginning."

Stay tuned for Book 2: *Interference*

The Married to the Game series

Discussion Questions

1. Do you think Gya had good intentions with her passion for serving God or was she the stereotypical 'judgmental Christian'?
2. Do you feel King should've completed his final year of college? If Tatum were your daughter, would you have advised her to drop out of school to maintain her relationship with King?
3. What are your thoughts about Tatum's mother, Vanessa?
4. Was it naïve of Gya to expect fidelity from Bryant, given his profession?
5. Were you sympathetic to Gya's heartache and trials or do you feel God was giving her a lesson in humility?
6. Was Tatum foolish to accept King's marriage proposal and believe he would change?
7. What are your thoughts about Bryant and his personal character?
8. Was Bryant justified in his feelings about Gya's intrusive social media presence or do you feel he should've been more supportive?
9. What part(s) of the book angered you?
10. Who is your favorite character? Least favorite?
11. Do you think Gya will go through with the divorce this time?
12. Do you believe King is guilty of the crime in which he is accused?

Author's Note

If you have enjoyed reading Game Time, I would greatly appreciate you leaving a review. Please follow me on my social media pages and join my private Facebook group, Sherron Elise's Reading Corner.

Let's stay connected! I always love to hear from readers and book clubs!

Website: www.sherronelise.com[1]

Email: sherronelise@gmail.com

Twitter: @sherronelise

Instagram: @sherronelise

Facebook: https://www.facebook.com/sherronelise

Private Facebook group: https://www.facebook.com/groups/sherronelisereadingcorner

As a bonus, I have included an excerpt from the first chapter of my debut novel, All That Glitters. Enjoy!

---

1. http://www.sherronelise.com

All That Glitters Excerpt

Chapter One: Racquel

"Racquel, are you ready? I'm walking out the door." Victoria Spencer said as she rummaged around in her closet for her other high heeled shoe.

"Really? You're walking out the door while still looking for your shoes?" Racquel kidded as she walked into her mother's spacious bedroom. Racquel was dressed to impress for Sunday morning church service in a pinstriped black and white Donna Karan pantsuit, the scent of Chanel No. 5 emanating from her neck and earlobes.

"You know what I meant, don't be cute," Victoria said wryly. "I know how you are with all of that primping. As soon as I get this shoe on I'm ready to go and I didn't want you holding me up."

"I come by it honestly! You're the queen of primping. Mom, you change *three* times before settling on an outfit, take an hour to do your make-up and another hour and a half to curl your hair."

"Stop exaggerating, Rocky. You know it doesn't take me an hour and a half to curl my hair, girl." Victoria said. This was true given that Victoria was a hair styling extraordinaire. She was owner and operator of Victorious Lockes, a salon she'd opened when Racquel was ten years old with the help of money she'd received in her divorce settlement from Racquel's father.

"But I see you didn't deny the outfits and make-up." Racquel said with a devious grin. She loved digging at her mother.

Victoria finally retrieved the elusive high heel and threw it in her direction.

It was important for Racquel to get her mother in a jovial mood considering the news she was about to break to her.

Racquel picked up the heel and sighed. "I bet you're going to miss those shoe discounts at Nordstrom's huh?" she said, her tone filled with feigned wistfulness.

Victoria paused in front of the full length mirror where she'd been giving herself a final once over. "What do you mean?" she asked with narrowed eyes.

Racquel looked at her in mock confusion. "You don't remember that I told you I quit Nordstrom's last Friday."

"No you *didn't* tell me you quit *anything.*" Victoria said, her voice escalating.

"Mom, yes I did!" Racquel continued to lie. "I came into the salon Friday night after I turned in my resignation. But it was so hectic in there you don't even remember. You know how busy Friday evenings are for you."

"Racquel, keep trying to play me for a fool, hear? I wasn't busy enough to forget something like that *had* you told me. This is getting ridiculous, Racquel. You've been quitting jobs on a whim since high school. I swear you haven't held down a job longer than three months." Victoria said.

"Mom, I was at Nordstrom's for six months." Racquel argued.

"It doesn't matter! I've had my salon for almost twelve years. I've been styling hair before you were born. All of that job hopping was fine and dandy in high school, Racquel, but you're about to graduate college. It's past time that you start developing a stable work ethic and more responsibility." Victoria said. She picked up a brush and ran it furiously through her bob. Her hair was full of body and bounced with each vicious stroke of the brush. She sucked her teeth. "I know it's partly my fault though. I was just talking to your father the other day about how I've spoiled and sheltered you."

Racquel grimaced at the mention of *him.* What was her mom talking to that bum about her for anyway? Racquel only spoke with him sporadically and saw him even less, mostly for the holidays.

"C'mon, Mom, it's not like I was going to make a career out of working at Nordstrom's or any of those other jobs. Besides, I'm trying to get an internship this year. I was going to end up leaving Nordstrom's regardless." Racquel tried to reason.

"You honestly believe you're going to secure a news reporting position as soon as you graduate? Racquel, times aren't like they were when I was growing up. Trust me, you're gonna wish you had that job at Nordstrom's when you graduate next spring and are unable to secure a job fresh out of college. You're turning your nose up at working as a sales associate but some of those associates at high end retailers earn pretty decent salaries." Victoria said, as if she were talking to an idiot. "Besides, I've been advising you to get an internship since your sophomore year. But silly me, I forgot. You kept changing your major. The word 'stability' doesn't seem to be anywhere within your mental rolodex."

Racquel rolled her eyes, albeit carefully because she knew her mother would've slammed her head clean through the full length mirror had she caught her. She was well aware that most internships didn't pay and there was no way she would spend her summers working for free. Sure, she'd quit jobs after a few months due to boredom or burn out, but at least she had enough sense to always save a little nest egg that would tide her over until she found another gig.

Racquel handed Victoria the heel she'd been holding so she could slide it on. She stood next to her mother at the mirror and took in both of their reflections. Despite her features being set in a terse expression due to her annoyance at Racquel, Victoria Spencer was a very attractive forty-six year old woman. Her vanilla pudding skin tone and features resembled the late R&B singer Vesta Williams.

Racquel, on the other hand, had a Hershey brown skin tone that she inherited from her father. She was indeed a feminine version of Wellington Spencer with high cheekbones that were framed by full and lustrous hair falling past her shoulders. She'd also acquired his coffee brown eyes.

They silently walked out to the garage and climbed inside of Victoria's silver 750Li BMW. Her mother turned on the radio and searched through the satellite stations for some Sunday morning inspiration. She came upon Walter Hawkins' *Going Up Yonder*. The gospel song blared through the speakers of the car and her mother hummed along as she drove. Racquel wanted to engage her in conversation, but she knew Victoria was probably still heated so it would be in her best interest to remain quiet.

The parking lot of Spiritual Pathway Church was already filling up for the eight a.m. service. The shrill sounds of police whistles resonated as they directed traffic and Victoria steered her vehicle through the orange cones that sectioned off different areas of the parking lot, making navigation somewhat easier.

Spiritual Pathway, founded by Pastor Angelique Healey, was well on its way towards becoming another of Houston's megachurches. Its five thousand square foot sanctuary could no longer house the membership that was well over a thousand parishioners, so Pastor Healey now held an 8 a.m. and 10 a.m. service to accommodate the expansion. The church was also in talks on whether to add on more space to the existing facility or build another larger church.

The beep of a car horn caught Racquel's attention as her mother pulled into a parking space. Her best friend Sydney Shephard whizzed by in her Mercedes with her mother, Nanette, in the passenger seat. Sydney pulled into a space a few cars down from theirs. Racquel watched as Sydney gracefully stepped out of her vehicle looking like a dead ringer for the actress Nia Long with her short, cropped haircut and glowing bronze skin. Her eyebrows were waxed to perfection, accentuating her almond brown eyes. A sleek forest green skirt suit hugged the curves of her petite form.

Sydney Shephard was the wife of Houston Meteor football player Gabriel Shephard. The two met while Sydney was an intern for the events department of the MetLife stadium in New York. The internship was in conjunction with the marketing degree she was studying for at Columbia University. Gabriel was playing for the New York Giants during that time. As Sydney and her mother strode toward them, Racquel felt the usual twist of envy that always emerged whenever she was in Sydney's presence.

It was envy that first manifested when Sydney called Racquel with the news of meeting the 6'1, 214 pound wide receiver. The envy that boiled over when Sydney described all of the exotic vacations taken with her new famous beau, in addition to all of the celebrities she had the pleasure of mixing and mingling with. The envy that finally exploded like a *meteor* hitting earth when Sydney flashed the rock in Racquel's face and gleefully announced their engagement.

Yet Racquel put on a happy face for her friend and stepped into her role as maid of honor, assisting Nanette with the preparation and hosting of a bridal shower for Sydney at Houston's Four Seasons Hotel. She kept the same happy face plastered on as she stood front and center watching Sydney and Gabriel exchange their vows at New York's opulent Oheka Castle.

Racquel always told herself she was being silly. It was only a matter of time before she nailed a millionaire of her own. Sydney and Gabriel had only been married for a little over a year and Racquel was practically joined at Sydney's hip whenever she had a team event or celebrity party to attend. Racquel even tried out for the Houston Meteorettes cheering squad and was livid when she wasn't selected, considering her years of cheerleading and ballet experience. Racquel also faulted Sydney, feeling that her friend could've had Gabriel pull some strings to get her on the squad. But she felt better once Sydney pointed out the Meteorette's non-fraternization rule that forbid them from dating the players. That stipulation defeated her purpose.

Now Racquel smiled when Sydney and Nanette finally reached them. "Don't forget to watch my baby on T.V. tonight before the Meteors and Steelers game." Nanette blurted out.

Racquel tried to keep from rolling her eyes. *Hello to you too, Miss Nanette,* she thought. *How could we forget?* Nanette nearly ran the clients and stylists crazy last Friday evening at the salon, going on and on about Sydney and Gabriel. But this was nothing unusual because that's all she talked about whenever she came in to get her hair styled. Ironically, Sydney was more humble than her mother. All Nanette ever did was brag and she was starting to make Racquel sick, living vicariously through her daughter. She also felt that Nanette took secret pleasure in the fact that Sydney snagged a good husband before Racquel did.

The television special Nanette was alluding to would showcase the nuptials of Jarad and Melodie Rolands. Jarad was a star forward for the Houston Asteroids and Sydney was merely being featured as the event planner for their wedding, which had taken place that past June.

"This is gonna be such good exposure for Sydney to launch her event planning company." Nanette went on.

Racquel smirked. Though she'd never admit it, Racquel suspected that it bothered Nanette that Sydney chose not to finish college. Nanette was really pushing the whole event planning thing so that Sydney wouldn't fall into the stigma of being just another trophy wife. She wanted to ensure that Sydney had some sort of identity. But Racquel thought she was a fool. Had the roles been reversed she too would've dropped out of college and became a wealthy housewife without a second thought.

"I'll definitely tune in. I'm so proud you, Sydney." Victoria said sincerely. "Maybe some of that drive will rub off on your friend over here and get her to stop quitting jobs

Racquel's blood boiled and she shot her mother a look of death.

"You quit Nordstrom's? I thought you liked it there. Girl, your company discount was sick. Shoot, I'm gonna miss that." Sydney joked.

"Now Syd, you know you could buy out Nordstrom's if you wanted to. Don't be silly." Nanette said.

Racquel wanted to punch her in her smug face and she wanted to punch her mother too. *You mean Gabriel could buy out Nordstrom's. Neither you nor Sydney would have a dime to your names if it weren't for him*, she thought wickedly. But she reminded herself she was in the midst of walking into the house of the Lord and checked her attitude.

"Yeah, I quit, but I want to focus on getting an internship." Racquel finally spoke up as they all walked towards the entrance of the church. "I've sent my resume to the local ABC, CBS, and NBC affiliates. Just think Sydney, one day I'll be on the air doing a lead-in to the Houston Meteor sports segment." Racquel said, referring to her desire to become a news anchorwoman.

The Spiritual Pathway grand lobby was packed with parishioners slowly trailing into the sanctuary for Youth Sunday, their voices echoing off the lobby walls. Those voices soon became drowned out by the youth choir as they belted out a rendition of Jonathan Nelson's *My Name is Victory*.

They found seats as close to the front as possible which was actually somewhere in the middle. As Racquel took her seat she observed the tall and statuesque Pastor Healey entering the pulpit flanked by her ministry team and armor bearer. The Pastor stood regal in a purple and white robe, her hair in its usual style of microbraids. A loyal client of Victoria's, Pastor Healey revealed that the braids were convenient for her fast paced life as a full time minister. She kneeled briefly before her seat in a moment of prayer before resuming her stance and clapping and swaying along with the choir. After the spirit filled praise and worship segment, the church announcements were read, followed by the collection of tithes and offerings. Racquel noted how they'd recently moved this portion of the service up. Initially, the collection took place after Pastor Healey's sermons. But due to the many people that would duck out of service early, it was now taken prior to the choir rendering its selections, afterwhich Pastor Healey would take the podium.

The lively choir was primarily the only part of the service Racquel enjoyed, along with the benediction. She always tuned Pastor Healey out and struggled to keep herself from nodding off by thinking about how she'd spend the rest of her Sunday and what she would wear to school that week.

After paying what would be her last tithe for awhile, and placing one dollar into the offering bucket, Racquel settled in to listen to the youth choir render its A&B selections. They began with Marvin Sapp's *Thirsty* which was led by Harmony Eubanks, a young butterscotch toned girl with beautiful and glossy shoulder length hair. Harmony was a stand out in the youth choir and sang lead on several songs, in addition to many solos. She had a delicate and angelic soprano voice that was reminiscent of Whitney Houston. Racquel recalled that Harmony had recently graduated from high school and she, along with many other graduates throughout the congregation, had been presented with congratulatory monetary gifts. All monies were donated through members of the church. Spiritual Pathway recognized all graduates each year in this fashion and Racquel couldn't wait until it was her turn. *College* graduates received up to $500. She was already imagining which stores she'd hit up at Houston's Galleria Mall.

Racquel realized she'd let her mind wander when she saw Pastor Healey take the podium with her Bible in hand. She racked her brain to try and remember the last song the choir had sung. Something to the effect of *I give myself away Lord so you can use me.* Racquel did recall Sydney becoming quite emotional, her hands stretched out in praise and crying softly. Sydney was now diligently taking notes as Pastor Healey spoke. Racquel noticed she seemed to be on a real religious kick as of late. She couldn't understand where this new Mother Theresa attitude stemmed from. She was definitely anything but virginal prior to meeting Gabriel. Sydney wasn't what you would call promiscuous but she definitely knew how to party. She wondered if this change was some put-on for Gabriel's sake to make him think he had the ideal wife.

Racquel was relieved when Pastor Healey wrapped up. She concluded with an altar call for prayer. The first service came to a close shortly thereafter.

"Victoria!" they heard a baritone voice call as they prepared to exit the sanctuary.

Racquel looked over her shoulder and suppressed a groan. It was Deacon Gordon Knowles, an older Idris Elba look alike with salt and pepper gray hair who Racquel suspected had a thing for her mother.

"Well, hello, Gordon!" Victoria said, with more enthusiasm than Racquel thought was necessary.

"And how are you, Racquel?" Gordon asked with a smile.

"I'm fine, sir, and yourself?" Racquel replied with a false politeness she hoped came off as sincere.

Gordon spoke to Nanette and Sydney as well. "We gonna stomp them Steelers tonight aren't we, Sydney?"

Racquel sighed inwardly, already seeing where the conversation was heading.

Gordon turned to the high yellow man standing next to him. "Raymond, this is Gabriel Shephard's wife. Everyone, this is my brother in ministry, Raymond Cunningham. He's just relocated to Houston from Shreveport."

"Oh, my husband Gabriel is from Shreveport." Sydney said.

"Yeah I know!" This Raymond person perked up. "We are mighty proud of that boy. I'm a huge fan." He shook Sydney's hand wildly as if she were Gabriel himself.

"Why, thank you." Sydney said, and smiled kindly.

"Raymond was the director of music at his church home in Shreveport. I'm going to talk to Pastor Healey about him filling in the recently vacated music director spot here." Gordon explained. The former music director had resigned once he'd gotten a deal with a record label.

"Well we look forward to seeing you in that role, Raymond." Victoria said.

"How about sooner? We were hoping you two ladies would join us for brunch." Gordon said, looking at her and Nanette.

Good, a man of her own is just what Nanette needs to stay out of Sydney and Gabriel's business, Racquel thought.

"That sounds great. Your treat right?" Victoria kidded.

"But of course." Gordon smiled.

"Where did you have in mind?" Victoria asked.

"Your call." Gordon replied.

"How about the Breakfast Klub?" she suggested.

"Vic that place is always so cramped and crowded." Nanette protested.

"That's because they have some awesome food." Victoria pointed out.

"Boy, my mouth is watering already." Raymond grinned.

"Raymond, you have to try their catfish and grits." Victoria said.

Racquel tuned them out, still mulling over Nanette's last remark. *The Breakfast Klub isn't classy enough for you? The nerve of this broad trying to act all brand new.*

"Nanette, you can ride with me. We'll meet you guys there." Victoria said to Gordon. "Oh, I'm sorry, Sydney, do you mind giving Rocky a ride home?"

"Of course not, Miss Vicki. Y'all go ahead and enjoy yourselves. I'll see you later, Mom. Call me tonight." Sydney said.

"I'll call you as soon as the special goes off. Raymond and Gordon I have to tell you all about my baby being featured on television tonight." Nanette said.

Oh Gawd! Is she serious? She's gonna run that poor man off already, Racquel thought in disgust.

Everyone bid one another goodbye and Racquel followed Sydney out to the parking lot.

"Hey, I'm pretty hungry too. Why not have brunch ourselves?" Sydney suggested.

"Not at the Breakfast Klub. I don't want to crash their dates." Racquel said.

"No, how about Mikki's Soul Food Café on West Bellfort?"

"Cool. I have a taste for their baked chicken and broccoli and rice casserole." Racquel agreed.

The two childhood friends made the drive to the cozy storefront restaurant on the Southwest side of Houston. Since it was still rather early the serving line wasn't wrapped outside the door as was the norm on Sunday afternoons. Many churchgoers made their way to the popular eatery after services. Racquel ordered baked chicken, broccoli and rice casserole and candied yams. Sydney had the smothered pork chops with rice and gravy and green beans. Each received complimentary cornbread muffins. Once getting some sweet tea to wash down their delicious meals, the ladies picked up their trays and made their way to a table.

"Okay, now that the preseason is underway, you found any potential teammates for me yet?" Racquel asked, as they dug in.

Sydney rolled her eyes in exasperation. "Rocky, please. I have better things to do than play cupid for you."

"Such as what, you modern day Donna Reed? No, scratch that. You don't qualify as a homemaker like Donna Reed. You have a maid and no kids."

"*Well*, we've definitely been working on that last part." Sydney said with a sly grin.

Racquel frowned. "So soon?"

Now it was Sydney's turn to frown. "What do you mean? We've been married for over a year."

"That's still practically the honeymoon phase though. I'd personally wait at least five years. Statistics claim that most marriages only last for that long. I figure if me and hubby can make it to the five year mark, then we're good to start a family." Racquel said.

Sydney waved her off. "Girl, aint nobody waiting no five years to have kids."

"I refuse to have my child be a product of divorce and end up a single parent like my mom and yours. And notice I said *child*, as in singular. I only want one. A little girl, a mini-me with her mama's swag." Racquel snapped her fingers and gave a little sway of her hips.

"Besides, "she continued, "I don't know why you're in such a rush. I read an interview given by another pro athlete wife, I forget her name. She said her husband spends so much time on the road that it's like being a single mother."

"Goodness, Racquel, why must you always be so negative?" Sydney said irritably.

Racquel jerked her head back. "Well lookie here at Miss *Attitude*."

"I'd just like to be able to hang out with you without us always talking about hooking you up with some dude, or about my marriage. Who I married doesn't define me as a person. I really expected that you, as my best friend, would understand that. And not change towards me."

Racquel sipped her tea, looking thoughtful. "I just feel...I don't know. It's almost like we don't have much in common anymore."

"Racquel I'm still the same Sydney."

"No. You're not. You'd *like* to be. But you're a married woman now. Married to a high profile man at that. I'm a college student still living at home with her mom."

"The dynamic between us will only change if you allow it to." Sydney said firmly.

"Okay. And I'll make an effort to stop riding you about securing me a baller. Now, let's talk about shopping."

Sydney laughed. "Now that's one thing we'll forever have in common."

Racquel leaned forward. "Girl I saw the baddest six inch heels..."

***

Racquel waved as Sydney tooted her horn and pulled off. She entered the house to find it empty. Her mother still hadn't returned from her lunch date. *Humph, they must be hitting it off pretty well*, she thought.

As she walked upstairs to her room, Racquel reflected back on her lunch date with Sydney, thinking about how her friend had some nerve trying to get all snippy with her. Racquel wasn't buying the phony modest act about her new lifestyle.

"*I'm the same Sydney,*" she mimicked to herself as she stepped out of her church attire. She sucked her teeth. "Yeah. Whatever."

Racquel powered on her laptop and decided to indulge in her guilty pleasure, which was chatting on a website called Jezcapades. It was a private chat room that required a $100 monthly subscription. Jezcapades was populated by women who, under anonymous online screen names, detailed their exploits with rich and wealthy men. But oftentimes the chats would consist of random conversation about their day-to-day lives, current events and other miscellaneous topics. Once the site's homescreen popped up she typed in her username and password and was brought to the site's welcoming screen:

THANK YOU FOR LOGGING IN, LADI OF LUXURY! ENJOY YOUR CHAT SESSION

Once at the main chat room screen, Racquel recognized some of the chatters already logged on. She greeted everyone and began to chat casually about her day.

Purchase the full book: https://books2read.com/u/3y1ExB

Don't miss out!

Visit the website below and you can sign up to receive emails whenever Sherron Elise publishes a new book. There's no charge and no obligation.

https://books2read.com/r/B-A-BGFT-LXYZB

BOOKS 2 READ

Connecting independent readers to independent writers.

About the Author

Sherron Elise is a proud native of Houston, Texas. An avid reader since childhood, her passion for getting lost within the pages of a book soon transformed into using her vivid imagination to create stories of her own. For more information about Sherron Elise you can visit her website at www.sherronelise.com and subscribe to her podcast, The College Christian Chat, available on Apple, Spotify, and other listening platforms.

Read more at https://sherronelise.com/.